Campus Life:

First Term

Kelvin Young

Cover art created by rockingbookcovers.com

Edited by Karen Meeus Editing

Dedication

This is for my husband.

And for all who've taken the time to read my story, thank you.

I hope you enjoyed reading it as much as I enjoyed writing it!

Table of Contents

Chapter 1

"Why do we live like this?" Andrew asked, throwing up his hands as Cassie stormed from the kitchen.

"If you don't like your *situation,* then you know where the door is!" she screamed as the door slammed with a final, resounding thud.

Leaning his head back and closing his eyes, he tried to relax himself and his nerves. Taking a deep breath, filling his lungs from bottom to top, he slowly exhaled long and deep.

"What, the actual, fuck?" Andrew whispered as he turned around and looked at the dishes in the sink. He didn't understand why it always came down to a fight with her. They'd been together for senior year and two years of junior college before moving to university. Everything had been copacetic until they'd moved in together last month.

"Test drive before you buy, son," his grandpa had told him before he moved away. "Know what you are getting into because love changes when the situation changes."

He shakes his head with a smile at the memory of his grandpa. He was the most loving, quiet, but steadfast person Andrew had ever met. Any time something happened, you always ran to Grandpa for protection because Gramma was sure to beat your ass. She'd been the keeper of the rules, *her* rules, and the entire family followed them. She was the kind of woman that would stand up for her family. She'd stand behind you and defend you until her last breath. That was unless you were in the wrong, and then she'd been the first to bust your ass from here till kingdom come.

Andrew often reflected on his grandparents and their relationship and how he wanted what they'd had. He wanted to be just like his grampa, hiking through the woods with his grandkids around the summer cabin and teaching them how to fish and skate on the frozen pond.

He thought he'd found that in Cassie and was sure they would be together forever, but his grandpa had been more than right. Subtle changes had started the moment that they'd moved in together. He'd come home from school, and she'd still be in bed, having missed the whole day of classes and sometimes work. From the first week of school, she'd coax him to help her with her homework until he'd tried to stop it. Then, she accused him of trying to sabotage her college career.

Shaking his head to get the thoughts from his head, he pushed it all away. He could sit here and ponder the great memories of his grandparents and how awful he was feeling in this situation, but it would not help him figure out what he needed in life.

The dishes were done, his homework was completed, and the house was picked up before he walked down the small hall to the bedroom. Listening at the door for a moment, he heard Cassie muttering, and he wondered if she was still angry.

He knocked on the door hesitantly, so soft it was barely audible. "Hey, Cass—"

"Go away!" she yelled through the wall.

"Want to hit up the quad for some dinner?"

"No, I don't! Can't you tell I'm on the phone?"

Like, how am I to know that with the door closed? Andrew thought. "Well, I'm going down to the quad if you want to come with me."

Grabbing a book, Andrew left and walked the paved trails to the college quad. It was a large area between several dorms and the cafeteria. The center had a fountain where the upper class would throw a bottle of Dawn at the end of school. The student ambassadors told the freshmen at orientation, and they warned the incoming student body that the campus police monitored it. The university had installed several cameras to catch possible future culprits, and they would be denied graduation.

That'd be awful, Andrew thought. To go through your entire college education just to be denied at the last moment over a bottle of Dawn soap. He chuckled and shook his head at people's stupidity.

The college had installed three sand volleyball courts on one side of the quad. Since the rec building was across campus from the dorms, the university implemented some changes to give students something recreational closer to the dorms. With the sand volleyball courts full, the campus set aside an area for outdoor recs and had just posted plans for a pickleball court and other activities they'd implement long term.

The sun was blazing bright, but a breeze kept the end of the summer cool. Andrew found a bench beneath one of the cherry blossom trees to read and people-watch. He was an hour into his book, and it was just getting good, when half the quad went wild. Looking up, he noticed a crowd had gathered around the court closest to him, and they were going crazy.

He rolled his eyes at the frat people, but their enthusiasm to be alive and have fun made him smile. Part of him wished he was in there having fun with them, but then again, he wasn't athletic.

Getting back to his book, he tried to ignore the crowd of people when a "Hey, watch out!" was the precursor to the volleyball that slammed into the side of his head, sending him off the bench and onto the stone ground.

"Holy fuck, guy! You okay?" someone said above him.

Everything was a little hazy and disoriented, and the words were barely getting through the ringing in his ears.

"Damn, that dude took it hard!"

"Knocked him clear off the bench!"

"He's gonna feel that shit tomorrow!"

All the voices and sounds blended in a cacophony of noise as if one were flipping the radio stations in the car too fast. He was lying on his side, tucked into the fetal position, with a hand covering his ear, which throbbed with every beat of his heart.

"Hey, you okay?" someone above him asked. "Here, let me see."

Gentle hands took hold of the hand that covered his ear. That hand wrapped around his and gently uncovered the side of his head.

"That smarts, doesn't it? Your ear is bright red, but there is no bleeding."

Slowly rolling onto his back, Andrew looked up at the guy above him. Bright sun rays beamed behind him, covering his face in shadow as if an archangel had come down from heaven. Translucent stone-gray eyes met him, and Andrew forgot some of the pain. He'd never seen eyes that color before.

"What the fuck happened to you?" The heavenly moment was interrupted by *her* voice.

Glancing to the right, Cassie stood with her hands on her hips and a sarcastic smirk on her pretty face. That look used to be one of amusement for some crazy or silly antic that he'd performed to bring out a smile. Now, he associated that smile with something completely different.

Then he saw the guy standing just a few feet behind her. Andrew had seen him sporadically around campus, and the stranger always seemed to make eye contact and smirk as if he knew something that no one else did.

"He took a blow to the head pretty good," the guy above him said. "Here, let me help you up." He took Andrew's hand and pulled him to his unsteady feet. "You able to stand, or do you need to sit?"

"Come on, Connor! Get the ball, and let's go," someone yelled behind them on the sand court. The sound seemed to echo through the quad.

"Here." Connor started to move so Andrew could sit on the bench.

"No, no, I'm okay," Andrew said after staring in a daze. "I'll be fine. I was just caught off guard, that's all."

"Caught off guard? More like knocked the hell out." Cassie chuckled, at which Connor looked at her as if she'd grown a second head.

"Well, if you need anything, just holler. I'll be on the court over there. Name's Connor," he said, giving Andrew a quick hand squeeze and a cheerful smile.

"Thanks, man," Andrew said.

"Yeah, no problem." With that, Connor ran back to the sand court.

"Seriously? You weren't even playing, and you got hurt," Cassie's sarcasm wrapped around him as she scolded him. "I knew you weren't athletic, but damn, I didn't know you were that pathetic with balls. Besides, I thought you were going to grab a bite to eat?"

"Decided to get some rays and pages in before the sun went down."

"Well, let's go, I'm hungry. Besides, we have to be up early tomorrow, and we haven't packed yet."

"For what?" Andrew asked, following her. He reached up gingerly, touching his throbbing ear with a slight wince.

"The float trip." She threw her hands up in irritated exasperation.

Knowing she hadn't told him about the float, he kept the peace and said, "Ah, that's right, the float. Must've forgotten."

The following day, they were up early to load the car with their cooler full of beer, water, premade sandwiches, and a dry bag for towels and spare clothes. They drove silently for almost two hours until they arrived at the river. The parking lot was already full of cars. College kids milled about talking and calling out to each other as they ran through the crowd in early morning antics. Some were already toasting their beers or drinks of choice when another screamed out, "Social," followed by the several who cheered the day. Unloading the car onto the bus was a feat since Cass had jumped from the car and then started talking to the guy who'd stood behind her yesterday. Andrew didn't miss the fact she hadn't said a single word to him all morning, but now Cassie was laughing and slapping that guy's arm in the playful way she used to treat him; they walked off.

Andrew grunted as he put the dry bag on the cooler and carried it all to the bus that drove them up the river several miles. The bus was full of people stuffed inside like a sardine can. The noise level from everyone screaming back and forth, country music blaring on someone's speaker, and the sounds of beer cans popping was a little much for so early in the morning. The bus had pulled off the road onto an old loggin' trail to get to the river, and the driver took the unpaved path like an Indy 500 racecar driver.

Thrown back and forth, Andrew gripped the seat in front of him, trying to keep off the guy he'd sat down next to. He'd tried to get a seat with Cassie, but she was farther back, and the bus had been too full to climb over everyone—besides, she was already sitting next to the guy from the day before.

"It's almost like you're on a mechanical bull!" the guy next to Andrew yelled to his buddies.

"Or the blonde from last night," a friend screamed in reply, bringing a round of howls, cheers, and grunts of approval.

"Good day for a float!" the guy across the aisle said. Andrew smiled and nodded at the one seemingly calm person on the bus beside him, and that was right before the stranger raised his beer, yelling at the top of his lungs, "Drink up bitches!!"

The bus went wild.

Not soon enough for Andrew, they arrived at the gravel bar, and the boats were filling up with coolers and college kids. Retrieving their cooler, Andrew found the boat Cassie had picked out with several people she seemed to know as they laughed and joked around.

"Hey." He smiled at her, climbing into the boat.

"Yeah?"

"Nothing." Andrew shook his head slightly and took out a beer for her and him.

The river was up, and the float was going faster than usual for this time of the year. With all the late-season rain, there was very little paddling or walking. They stopped several times to get in some swimming in the deeper waterholes while others were playing flag football on the rocky shores. Not knowing anyone except Cassie, Andrew hung out on the boat and sunned on the raft.

The river bank was full of activity. Across the river, people yelled as they swung out on a rope swing, while others drifting by on rafts called out to friends, and the guys on the gravel bar jeered and hollered to each other. The noise made the whole experience very overwhelming. Andrew never considered himself anti-social, but he wasn't one to put himself out there either. He preferred a smaller group of friends in a quieter atmosphere. Since he'd moved to college, he'd immersed himself in classes and studies and had not met many new people or made friends.

Laying on the side of the raft enjoying the heat and the sun, Andrew was stretching when a "Watch out!" reached him, and a football dive-bombed into his stomach with a resonating *thwack*!

Andrew's legs jerked up to cover his stomach, and he rolled off the raft. Unceremoniously, he landed on his face and knees on the rocks as he vomited.

"Fuckin nasty."

"Someone's drank too much," someone from across the river yelled as he pointed and laughed.

"Seriously? Someone wash off the ball."

"Dude, you okay?" said a familiar voice above him. A voice accompanied by a comforting hand on his naked back. A voice he remembered but could not grasp from where because of the pain that wracked his abdomen.

"You just seem to be attracting balls lately." Cassie drunkenly sniggered, reaching into the cooler for another beer for her and her friend.

Another wave of nausea coursed through him, along with a dry heave.

"Hey, Drew, you okay? Want me to get some water to wash that taste from your mouth?"

"Hey, Connor! Are you coming or what?"

"Naw, go ahead. I'll catch up later," Connor called back with a wave to the footballers before he leaned down to look at Andrew. "Hey, here's some water when you are ready. It'll help." He rubbed Andrew's back comfortingly as a parent would a child's.

"Trying to catch my breath," Andrew stammered. he pushed up from the rocks after a few gulps of air and tried to swallow the heaves that threatened to make their way back up. A few scrapes from the fall were evident on his face.

"Dude, you took that hard," Connor said, sitting back. "Sorry, I didn't catch it."

"Not your fault, it happens," Andrew said, reaching for the water to rinse his mouth.

Connor helped Andrew up onto the side of the raft, and he jumped up a little with an "Ahh damn, that's hot!"

"Shit, sorry." Connor pulled him from the raft, and Andrew slid in the gravel, falling into Connor, who tried to steady them but slid on the gravel bar himself. They both fell backward into the cold river water.

"Fuck, that's cold." Andrew popped from the water. The pain from his stomach was forgotten, along with the burning sensation that initially drove them from the raft.

Connor surfaced laughing. Running one hand down his face to wipe the water away and the other through his brown hair to keep more water from running into his eyes. "Hey, man, sorry for that. That gravel—"

"All good, man," Connor chirped, and then he started walking from the water, Andrew following right behind him. When Andrew slipped again, Connor reached out and took his elbow. "Are you accident-prone or what?" He laughed.

"You've no idea." Andrew chuckled.

"I'm getting a good one!"

Climbing onto the riverbank, Connor grabbed two beers from a random cooler. "Here ya go, you've earned one of these."

"Thanks." Andrew popped the can and took a long swig. Lowering the can, he spied Cassie as she headed behind some bushes up the bank close to the tree line.

"That your girlfriend?" Connor asked.

"Yeah, we've been dating for almost three years. Probably just had to go pee." Andrew took a deep breath as they both watched the guy who'd been by her side earlier subtly walk around the opposite side of the brush.

Andrew looked at Connor, who tried to keep his face neutral. Andrew breathed and started toward the brushes at the back of the gravel bar. Gathering his resolve, he could feel his chest tighten as his anxiety increased. His breath came quicker, and he clenched his hands in anger.

He'd made a promise to Cassie before they came to college, and he'd been trying to keep that promise no matter how hard it became. No matter how much she was changing, he'd tried to change with her, but now he knew she was changing in a way he didn't want or like. She was using him, and she was treating him as if he were nothing.

He knew better than that. He knew his worth and realized she did not deserve the time or effort he gave her. She wasn't worth his affection.

He was so focused on his mission that he didn't hear the footsteps behind him. All he could see were the dense green bushes, hoping against hope that he was not going to find what he knew in his heart he was going to find.

Walking around the bushes, he came to a stop. There she was. His Cassie bent over a fallen tree with her swimsuit bottoms pulled to the side while that guy was behind her, thrusting for all he was worth.

Andrew's eyes narrowed in anger. He'd been seeing the signs over the last few days. He had his suspicions, but he'd refused to believe them. He'd felt the distance growing between them, a small rift that had grown into a chasm radiating a darkness he could not traverse.

He hadn't believed it at first, and then he hadn't wanted to believe it as he'd clung to the thought of what they once were—or had—but all the signs were there. He'd thought maybe it was college, or the stress of being away from home and her parents, the loss of friends from their hometown that forced them to make new ones, or the stress of their relationship since they'd moved in together for the first time.

Andrew wanted to yell, or scream, or . . . something to get back at her. He wanted—he didn't know what he wanted. He felt nothing while watching Cassie, but he knew he refused to live like this.

Drunken anger surged through him. He was not one to give in to rage or drunken impulse, but he'd had enough. She'd embarrassed him for the last time. His eyes narrowed, focusing on that lying, cheating, hoe.

Wobbling, he started to take a step forward when Connor grabbed him by the arm.

"Not worth it, man," Connor said, pulling him back. "Come on, let's get out of here."

Andrew turned to him. "And go where? Back to the boats until they're done fucking? Until she's done embarrassing me?"

Andrew looked back at them again. They were drunk and so involved in their fucking that they never realized he was there.

"No, Drew, we are getting out of here," Connor said as he pulled Andrew beside him. "There are some guys with a canoe. One of them owes me a favor for a paper I wrote for him. We'll take the canoe and get out of here."

"But you don't even know me." Andrew lagged while Connor pulled him across the gravel bank.

"No one needs that in their life, man. You are worth more, and I hope you know that."

As they made their way to the canoe, Connor briefly talked to his friend before signaling Andrew to get his stuff. Together, they loaded the cooler, climbed into the canoe, and started down the river—away from his old life.

Chapter 2

Andrew was silent for two miles on the river before venting loudly. Raging in anger at the whole situation, he'd unintentionally told Connor everything. They had met in their senior year of high school and stayed together through two years of junior college before moving to university. He named off flaws and times when she held him back. At one point, he started to cry, which could have been the beer or his pure anger, but then he wiped his eyes and clenched his fists. He bellowed down the river. His voice echoed through the river valley and the tree-covered banks, but at this point of the river, they were alone.

When they stopped to grab some sun in the water, rest their arms from rowing, and pee, Connor was given a surprise.

Standing waist-deep in the water with a cold beer and teary eyes, Andrew gazed as if in a daze at the water flowing all around him. "You know, we never had sex." He pursed his lips and nodded as if this was a moment of shame. "At first, she said she wanted to wait until marriage, and I respected that. No matter how frustrated I got, I had made a promise to her."

"Really?"

Andrew nodded, still not meeting Connor's eyes.

"Never?"

"Nope." Andrew looked to the sky and shook his head, embarrassed. "So, you can say that you have officially met a twenty-one-year-old virgin."

"Hey." Connor stepped forward and put a hand on his shoulder. "That is nothing to be ashamed of but something to celebrate. That you committed, and you never went back on that commitment. You don't have to throw your virginity away on someone who doesn't deserve it."

Andrew's dark-brown eyes met Connor's stone-gray eyes. From this close, he could see the conviction behind them.

"You're just saying that." Andrew laughed, then took a drink, and Connor's hand fell from his shoulder. "Hot guy like you, bet girls have been all over you since primary school."

"Well, thank you, but this"—Connor motioned to his shoulders, pecs, and abs—"did not happen in high school but in college. From primary school until university, I was the ugly duckling. So, I relate a little more than you know."

"Really?" Andrew looked as if he wanted to apologize for being rude, but Connor stepped in.

"No need for all that. You are angry and expressing your frustrations, but please don't judge me until you get to know me. Then"—Connor caught his eye again—"you can judge all you want."

Andrew gave a slow, sad nod. "Sorry," he whispered.

"No need for that, but let's get going so they don't catch up to us."

Andrew was silent for the first hour of the car ride home and asleep for the last hour.

"Get your stuff," Connor said as he entered the dorm apartment.

"What?"

"You're not staying here." Connor walked to the bedroom, grabbed a clothes basket, and threw it on the bed.

"Where am I going to go? I don't have anywhere to stay," Andrew said, throwing his hands in the air.

"I've got a room you can stay in," Connor said. "My roommate moved out a few months ago, and I've been looking for someone to help pay the bills. I was about to hang up a sign on the quad bulletin boards, but this will save me a lot of time and money."

"You don't even know me." Andrew stood in the doorway.

"Are you a serial killer?"

"Uh, no."

"Do you steal? Lie? Cheat or have any other nefarious qualities?"

"Nefarious? Good use of the word." Andrew reluctantly chuckled.

"You have a job or are capable of getting one?" Andrew grinned. "I can't have a mooch living off me again like the last roomie."

"Yes." Andrew nodded.

"Then it's settled. You will stay with me. Even if it is a trial run and you want to move out later, you are not staying here," Connor said with finality, then started loading up the clothes basket. "Grab whatever you want or need. Obviously, you can come back later and get whatever else you need, but I'd rather you not have to see her again."

Andrew stared at Connor's back as he loaded another basket with clothes. His strong back muscles showed through the thin material of his shirt, and his slightly jerky movements conveyed his anger when he stood up and looked around for a moment.

"What else?" Connor asked. "I've all your clothes packed. Do you have anything else that you want or need?

"Why?" Andrew asked.

"Why what?"

"Why are you helping me?"

A sad smile crossed Connor's full lips, and his gray eyes looked down momentarily before meeting Andrew's dark-brown eyes with defiance.

"Because I know what it is like to have someone cheat on you, and I know how it feels to love someone who doesn't love you back."

They stood staring at each other for a long moment. Andrew could feel his anxiety start to rise, or a nervousness that he couldn't explain caused his pulse to quicken and his breath to hasten.

"I didn't have anyone but Becky to help me, and I knew I could help you," Connor said. "I could be your Becky."

"Thank you." Andrew looked down as tears escaped the sides of his eyes.

Connor took two steps across the room and wrapped his strong arms around Andrew. "It'll be okay," he whispered into Andrew's hair, placing his cheek atop his head.

Andrew felt the protection and warmth in that hug. He had not felt it for longer than he could remember. He used to feel like this when his dad would hug him, and he used to feel—no, he realized. He'd never felt that way about Cassie.

Nodding his head into Connor's chest, he murmured, "Okay, let's go."

Connor stepped back, took one of the baskets, and handed it to Andrew. Their hands touched for the briefest of moments, and Andrew felt like sparks shot through his fingers for that instant.

Four blocks from campus, Connor pulled into the drive of a three-story Victorian-style house. Andrew took in the large house with the manicured lawn and looked at Connor.

"You live here?" Andrew asked. "Seriously?"

Connor laughed at that. "Yeah, but it isn't all mine." He pulled the car around the house and into the garage. They got out of the car and unloaded the baskets of clothes, then went through a door and up two flights of stairs.

Entering a beautifully lit room, Andrew looked around. The single room was large, with an oversized couch directed toward a wall-mount flat screen. Behind the sofa was an island with chairs before the kitchen, two doors to either side of the kitchen, and just past the living room was a rounded space fit into the small tower built into the house. The rounded space was all windows and lush couches covered with throw pillows. Andrew walked over in a daze, looking around.

"That is always everyone's favorite space." Connor laughed. "Look up."

The room's vaulted ceiling, painted with a mural of several mythical creatures and gods, was lit by a stained glass lamp resting on a chain.

"This is amazing!" Andrew said in awe. "Did you do this?"

"Me? Hell to the no." Connor laughed. "My friend Becky is the artist."

"She's so talented!"

"Yeah, I think so too. Wait until you meet her. She's not like any artist you've ever met." Connor laughed, then headed toward the door to the right of the kitchen. "This will be your room," he said, then entered.

"Can I sleep out there?" Andrew joked as he reluctantly followed.

"Well, you might have to." Connor looked around the room for a moment. On one side of the room, there was a weight bench and a few weights stacked neatly in the corner, and on the other, there was a camera on a tripod, a white backdrop, and a large circular light.

"This will be your room," Connor amended. "Sorry, I'll have to move this stuff, and we can find a bed to put in here."

"Are you a photographer?" Andrew put the basket down and walked around the room, observing the photography equipment.

"No." Connor shook his head. "My old roommate was and has yet to come get this stuff. I was working out to get in shape"—Connor motioned to the weight bench—"and he was a photographer. So he took some photos and sent them in."

"Yeah?" Andrew looked at his new roommate with a smirk.

Connor laughed. "Yeah. The pictures sold, and I received some money, hence the house. I live here in the attic and have plans for the basement and two floors below. That's when everything went sideways."

Andrew looked at Connor, who shook his head and walked from the room. "Here," he called from the kitchen, and Andrew followed.

"There is an extra chest of drawers in my room. We can put your clothes there and figure out the sleeping arrangements until we get that stuff moved and a bed in there for you. We can bunk, or I can take the couch."

"I don't think you should be on the couch after all you've done for me," Andrew said.

"So bunk it is." Connor opened the door to his bedroom, and they both went in.

The room was huge. A king-size bed sat opposite the door and was flanked by two large windows. Two dressers sat opposite each other with an oversized, comfortable stuffed chair. Another door led to a large bathroom with a tile-encased walk-in shower just past the clawfoot tub and a double vanity.

"Damn, how much did those pictures sell for?" Andrew looked around the rooms.

"Enough," Connor smirked. "Here, we'll throw your clothes here and unpack you tomorrow. I think you need a long hot shower while I make us a little something for dinner, and then let's call it a night. It's been a seriously long day." He drew out the 'O' and rolled his eyes with a chuckle.

"Deal," Andrew said, retrieving his clothes basket from the other room. He went to the shower, stripped, and entered, then realized he had no idea how to work it. There were two showerheads above, six coming from the walls, and a panel of buttons instead of a knob.

He pushed a button or two, trying to figure it out when a loud noise emanated from the panel.

"Oh, here." Connor ran into the room and walked into the shower.

"Sorry." Andrew stepped back, then suddenly became very aware of his nakedness, the proximity of a shirtless Connor, and his penis that suddenly started to react.

"I should've shown you," Connor said while Andrew tried to put his hands in front of him without drawing notice. "Press here to start, and then—" But Andrew could not concentrate on anything except for the crease that ran down Connor's back and the muscles that flared out like a butterfly's wings.

His shorts were the shorty shorts that were European but suddenly so popular here in the States. Andrew could not take his eyes off the muscular globes beneath the stretched material of the shorts. His breathing picked up, and not for the first time, he started wondering about himself when Connor interrupted his thoughts with a, "Got it?" and looked at Andrew.

"Umm, I think so," Andrew said, trying not to meet Connor's eyes.

"Hey, no worries." Connor smiled. "Just like a locker room, yeah?" With a few quick movements, Connor had the shower up and running and walked from the room.

After a long, hot shower that seemed to wash the day's stink off him and the stink of Cassie from his life, Andrew made his way to the kitchen. The smells wafting through the bedroom were terrific, and Andrew realized he had not had anything to eat in too long as his stomach growled.

"Seriously?" Andrew said as he took a seat. "A sexy, rich model, probably a straight-A student, and you can cook?"

Connor laughed. "Don't judge it until you've tasted it."

"So you are a sexy, rich model?" Andrew chuckled.

"Well, rich enough and on the Dean's List. The rest is in the eye of the beholder." Connor smiled, and his stoney eyes seemed to sparkle. "Besides, you've not even tried it."

"I've smelled it. Anything that smells this good must be amazing!"

"Bet," Connor said with a cheerful grin.

"I'll be the judge," Andrew said, then reached for a fork. The smell of the baked chicken with mashed potatoes dressed up with green beans was heavenly until he took a bite. It was all Andrew could do to keep chewing. He tried to keep the nauseated look off his face, continued to chew, and swallowed like a trooper.

"Umm, good," he said, then reached for a glass of water.

"You don't have to lie." Connor grimaced.

"Um, I'm not," Andrew said around another drink from his glass.

Connor pouted. "Oh? Think you can do better?"

"We'll enjoy this." Andrew looked down at his plate with a pause, then back at his new roomie. "Lovely meal tonight. I'll cook breakfast."

"Deal." Connor reached his hand out, and Andrew looked at it, raising his eyebrows. "We'll shake on it."

Andrew took Connor's hand. It was rough but smooth at the same time. His grip was firm but not overpowering, and sparks seemed to shoot up his arm as they shook on the deal.

"Just so you know, if you are a better cook, then you must make all the meals," Connor teased.

"Oh, is that right?" Andrew took another bite, chewed, and swallowed hard.

"Yeah, that's right, Mr. 'I can cook better than you.' "

"What would it be worth?" Andrew asked with another drink to wash the overseasoned taste from his mouth.

"What is what worth?" Connor took a bite and then scrunched up his face.

"A good meal?" Andrew asked, grinning.

"All the tea in China." Connor laughed after another bite. "Seriously, if you can cook, you can stay for free!"

Andrew smiled a devious smile. "I went to cooking school," he announced.

"What?"

"My junior college before I came here. It was cooking school," Andrew told him.

Connor lowered his fork and narrowed his beautiful eyes. "I feel like you've been leading the witness, sir."

"Umm, but this chicken is so good . . ." Andrew and Connor burst into a fit of laughter.

Climbing into the large bed, Andrew tried to reflect on the day. It had been a long, hot, stressful, and emotionally charged day—a day of discovery and lessons learned. He tried to sort out his thoughts, but the sound of the shower and the comfortable bed were pulling him under.

He was startled awake when the door to the bathroom opened, and light shone into the room. He hadn't been asleep that long and had barely opened his eyes to see Connor walk from the bathroom naked. His breath caught in his chest as he watched him go to his dresser and take out a pair of briefs.

Connor told Alexa 'good night,' and the whole house seemed to shut down as he climbed into bed. Andrew rolled over, trying to figure out the thoughts that seemed to rush across his mind when sleep once again pulled him in.

Chapter 3

Andrew ran through the moonlit summer night with his friend Sean and Sean's brother, Jeremy. They were on a camping trip with Sean and Jeremy's dad, Steven, for a week of fishing and relaxation. They'd been out on the river all day, hiking all afternoon before returning to camp and making dinner.

After the meal, Steven announced that he was going to take a quick dip in the lake, and the boys stayed behind around the fire. Getting into the cooler, they found Steven's bottle of vodka and spiked their sodas before having another round. When Steven returned, he told them not to stay up too late and went into his tent.

After their third drink, the boys decided to take a swim. Running through the dark trees, the boys whooped louder than they realized as they stripped down. Once on the riverbank, they dropped their shirts; Sean and Andrew started forward when Jeremy told them to strip down completely. Both boys turned to him as he pulled down his shorts.

"What the fuck?" Sean asked his brother.

"You don't want to have to explain to Dad why everything is wet, do you? Think he'd be okay with us drinking and swimming in the dark without him knowing?" Jeremy asked and stepped out of his shorts.

"Dude!" Sean yelled at his brother, putting his hand up. "I don't wanna see your dick."

Andrew stood transfixed. Jeremy was only a year older than they were, but he was a lot bigger than he was. He watched Jeremy's thick cock swing back and forth, then bounce against his low-hanging balls in the moonlight as he started running for the water. Turning as Jeremy ran past, Andrew watched those perfect ass cheeks flex with each step.

Dropping his shorts, Andrew ran away from Sean and into the dark water before anyone noticed that he had a raging hard-on. He figured getting in with Sean behind him and Jeremy still underwater would be easier, and the darkness helped. He dove into the water, and Jeremy was yelling at his brother when he surfaced.

"Chicken shit!!"

"Gay boy," Sean shot back.

"What? You've never seen a dick in the locker room? Like I care anyway, you're my brother."

"Jealous that I'm bigger?"

"So you have been looking?" Jeremy yelled to the shore.

"Fuck off," Sean called back, and Jeremy flung water on the shore, getting his brother wet. "Fucker," came across the water as Sean's shorts hit the rocks and he ran into the water, tackling his brother.

Andrew stood frozen in the cold water, shocked at how big his friend Sean was. Both boys had full-grown cocks, and they weren't yet men themselves. The boys wrestled, splashed, called each other names, threw around insults, and then laughed as they wrestled naked in the dark water; all the while, Andrew watched them.

Jealous.

He was an only child, and he'd always wanted a sibling. He watched how they fought, picked on, badmouthed, and stood up for each other. He had always been jealous. They had always treated him as a long-lost brother, but he knew he wasn't, even though they tried.

A wave of water hit him in the face as Jeremy threw Sean further out into the water. Shaking the water from his face, Jeremy hollered, "Think you're getting out of this, huh?"

Rough hands grabbed him in the water. Andrew tried to twist away, but Jeremy pulled him closer and twisted him around. His wet arms seemed to be everywhere at once. Sean came up laughing and shouted, "Get him!!" all while a stunned Andrew stood with arms pinned over his head in a Full Nelson.

"Dude! You let him get you? I'm coming." Sean snickered, trying to rush through the dark water as fast as he could.

Andrew felt Jeremy's wet chest against his back and his hard dick rubbing against his butt cheeks. Realizing he was sporting a raging hard-on once again, he tried to twist from the other boy's hold as Jeremy chuckled in his ear, holding him tighter. Worried Sean would realize he was hard, Andrew struggled even harder, which caused Jeremy's erection to delve deeper between his ass cheeks.

Sean feigned right and then went around to the left, but Jeremy jerked him around, and Sean collided with them, and they all went down. Jeremy and Andrew surfaced as Sean jumped from the water with a laugh, holding his hand over his eye. "Fuck dude, I think you damned near took my eye out with that boner of yours!"

Andrew instantly turned red even though they couldn't see it in the dark. "Um," he mumbled.

"Surprised you could keep it up in this cold water." Sean sniggered. "Mine was like, 'Hey, umm nope, buh-bye.' " And he guffawed, dropping his hand from his face and splashing them.

"Boys!" their dad called, and all three of them turned toward the camp.

"Damn, you woke up the old man, screeching like a little girl." Jeremy splashed his brother.

"Did not."

"Yeah, well, it's your turn," Jeremy said.

"What? No! I went last time, damnit."

"Um, no, I went so you could stay with Brittany—"

"Damn." Sean splashed. "Fine, but you owe me."

"Sucker!" Jeremy laughed as they all started to climb out of the water.

Sean was the first on the shore, and Andrew got a good look at his muscular ass in the moonlight, which did nothing to make his still-hard dick go down.

"You're right." Jeremy laughed. "He could put an eye out with that! Damn, son."

Peals of laughter followed as Andrew tried to fall back into the dark water, accompanied by another call from their dad.

"Coming, coming." Sean rolled his eyes, pulled on his shorts, grabbed his shirt, and disappeared into the dark.

"Come on," Jeremy said as he climbed the riverbank. "We were just teasing."

"What'd Sean do with Brittany?" Andrew asked as he prayed to everything above to make his dick go down.

"He didn't tell you?" Jeremy asked. "He tells you everything!" Jeremy seemed genuinely flabbergasted.

"Apparently, not everything."

"Two weeks ago, when we were at the county fair, they hooked up behind the barn."

"What?" Andrew said, suddenly pissed. "Couldn't people see them?"

"Naw, they were between the hay bales and the barn, and besides, it was dusk. I covered for him so they could . . . Get. It. On!" He accentuated the words with a slap in the air as if he were smacking an ass.

"Dickweed," Andrew said and bent over to retrieve his shorts. As he bent down, he felt a suddenly familiar cock press into his ass.

"Speaking of getting it on," Jeremy said.

Andrew jerked up and spun around. Jeremy took Andrew's face in his hands, and their lips met. Andrew's eyes grew large, and they were met by Jeremy's dark eyes, which seemed to stare into his soul.

Taking a deep breath through his nose, Andrew started to relax and slowly closed his eyes, sinking into the kiss. Their mouths opened, and Andrew followed Jeremy's lead. His stomach twisted nervously as Jeremy pressed their bodies together.

Letting go of his face, Jeremy cupped the back of his neck so he couldn't pull away as another hand slid down Andrew's back and cupped an ass cheek. Jeremy pulled them together, and their dicks pressed and slid against each other's as the kissing went on. Both boys started gyrating their hips, increasing the friction between them.

The kiss became more natural when he wasn't concentrating on it. He'd never kissed anyone like this before, but it was doing something to his dick, and the movements between them felt so right. Jeremy's *hand squeezed that ass cheek he'd been holding on to, and his fingers started to sink into the crevice between—*

"Jeremy!!"

Steven's call from the tree line separated them, and the camping trip was suddenly over.

Andrew's eyes jerked open with a sudden snort from his sleep. Raising his head, he looked around, dazed and confused. The light coming into the room was foreign to him, and he realized he wasn't in his bedroom or his bed, and the person beneath him wasn't Cassie.

Looking up, he realized Connor was lying on his back with a hand draped over Andrew's shoulders; all this time, he'd had a leg across Connor's legs, and he was using Connor's chest as a pillow. Connor groaned in his sleep and turned his head away from Andrew but moved a leg into his crotch.

Andrew gasped at the realization he was sporting some major morning wood, which was now pressed into the other man's thigh. Embarrassed, he tried to extricate himself from the situation.

Slowly, Andrew drew his leg up and then gradually moved it back as he tried to pull his arm and body back simultaneously. It was as if he were in some weird yoga pose. He moved off Connor carefully, trying to keep the covers in place. He didn't want the cold air to rush in and wake his new roomie, and he didn't want his new roomie to know he'd been cuddling for all he was worth.

Silently, he climbed from the bed and turned toward the bathroom when the door to the bedroom slammed open.

"Connor!" A girl busted into the room, screeching at the top of her lungs.

"Ahh!" Andrew screamed at her, then fell backward onto the bed and rolled off the foot onto the floor.

Connor sat up wide-eyed, looking around like the troops were storming the beach without him.

Andrew jumped up from the floor. "What the fuck!"

"Damn, honey, are those board shorts because that is some serious wood! Holy hell," the girl said.

"Wow!"

Andrew's gaze snapped to Connor, who was staring at his crotch, before he threw his hands over himself and backed into the bathroom, slamming the door.

"Good job!" He could hear her through the door. "He's like a sexy librarian ready to pounce when you've returned the book late!"

"Becky!" Connor's mirth could barely be heard through the door, which Andrew was leaning against in embarrassment.

"Seriously! He's a hot little body, a full set of abs, that tousled brown hair to match his eyes—"

"You got all that just by scaring the shit out of him?" Connor snorted, and Andrew imagined a cute little smirk across Conner's pink lips.

"I'd have gotten that cock, too, if I'd have had another second. Jesus, son!"

"You're incorrigible, Bek." Andrew nodded his head in agreement at Becky's vulgarity. If her sole purpose was to stay so she could embarrass him, it was working.

"Now I see why you missed the Kitchen this morning," Becky's voice grew, then faded in volume as if she were pacing the room just past the door where Andrew stayed hidden.

"Ugh, that was this morning!" Connor clapped his hands into the comforter around him.

"Yeah, but trust me, no one is going to fault you for spending a little you time with you instead of taking care of everyone else!"

"Damn." Andrew heard Connor throw back the covers and the mattress ruffle as he climbed out of bed. "I hate to miss—"

"Bro! I didn't get the memo to wear my board shorts." Becky's giggling caused Andrew to smile. "Soldiers!! Ah-ten-tion!" She clipped her heels together, and he imagined her saluting in exaggeration.

Connor looked down, and a perfect outline showed through his briefs to his right hip.

"I feel overdressed, so call me!" And with that, she was gone.

"You can come out now," Connor called, and Andrew stuck his head out of the bathroom door, wide-eyed. "Sorry about that. We had a date this morning, and I must have slept through it."

"Is she always like that?" Andrew asked from the door.

"Yeah." Connor laughed as he flung the comforter up, letting it settle and then tugging to smooth it out. He turned to where Andrew's head was still poking from the door. His large brown eyes were focused on Connor's crotch.

"Sorry about that." Connor motioned to his perfect outline.

"I was right there with ya, it happens." Andrew laughed it off.

"Well, since we are in the same boat, want to shower the stink off before you make me the most amazing breakfast I've ever had in my life?"

"Together?"

"We do it in the locker room?" Connor shrugged.

"Sure." Andrew stepped back with a wary look as Connor entered the bathroom.

"Hot?"

"Thanks." Andrew put a hand behind his neck and rubbed his muscles while his arm flexed, showing a perfect bicep.

"I meant the water." Connor gave him a teasing smile. "You like the water hot?"

"Oh." Andrew looked around nervously, trying to keep his eyes anywhere but where they kept wanting to roam. "Yeah, I like it hot."

"Me too." Conner smiled again, sliding his briefs past his hips and letting them fall to the floor before stepping out of them.

Andrew felt his breath catch in his chest. Connor was a perfect specimen of an Adonis coming to life. Broad, muscular shoulders, high and tight pecs, abs that went on for days, muscled legs, and strong feet. But Andrew could not stop staring at his cock. It was chubbing up, but not hard. A perfect helmet head rested on large, full testicles and immaculately trimmed pubes.

"I understand why your pictures sold so well," Andrew blurted out.

"Thanks," Connor smirked at him. "Not too bad yourself, for a *sexy librarian*," he air-quoted Becky.

They both laughed, and Connor turned on all the shower heads. "You like all the heads?"

"Umm."

"Shower heads?" Connor amended.

"Down for whatever," Andrew said.

"Well, get those boxers down and get in here then. I'm getting hungry." Connor rubbed a strong, wet hand across his abs. "I'm wasting away to nothing! And I need my back washed."

Andrew suddenly grew self-conscious, knowing that Connor was watching him and watching intently. He knew that Connor was already naked, but with a body like that, Andrew would go *everywhere* naked!

With a shrug, Andrew dropped his underwear and stepped into the shower before he lost his nerve, on full display.

"Not bad." Connor's brows furrowed, and the corners of his lips pulled up in an appreciative smirk at the vision before him.

"Umm, thanks." Andrew chuckled nervously, then turned to close the door.

"Not bad at all!"

Andrew shook his head, then stepped under the showerheads. "Turn around, and I'll get your back, but you have to get mine."

"Deal, but then I want breakfast." Connor chuckled.

"Deal." Andrew returned with a wink. "I can hear you wasting away from here."

Chapter 4

The apartment was filled with the aromas of melted cheese, baked croissants, bacon, and thyme, along with Connor's approving sound when he took a bite of his breakfast sandwich.

"Seriously, how did you do this?" Connor said with a smile of appreciation.

"With love and a wooden spoon, of course." Andrew smiled as he watched Connor close his beautiful eyes and take another bite of the sandwich. His little sounds, how that little bit of croissant was in the corner of his mouth before he swallowed and ran his pink tongue around to get the crumb . . . Andrew was enraptured.

"What?" Connor asked, grinning. "Do I have something on my face?" He wiped his mouth.

"No, it's not that." Andrew took a bite of his sandwich and glanced away.

"What is it then?"

Andrew looked around the room and seemingly everywhere but at his new roomie.

Connor reached across the island's onyx countertop and took Andrew's smaller hand in his own, rough hand. "What is it?" His gray eyes bored into Andrew, who tried desperately not to meet them.

Andrew glanced down with a long exhale, and a tear escaped the corner of his eye. "It's just—" His Adam's apple bobbed momentarily as he tried to collect himself, and Connor gave his hand a squeeze of confidence. "It's just that it has been so long since anyone has had anything nice or appreciative to say about me."

Andrew watched through teary eyes as Connor sat back with a sigh of resignation. A look of what could be misconstrued as pity crossed those strong features before smoothing out. Slowly, Connor stood and walked around the counter. Connor took Andrew in his strong arms and hugged him.

Warmth and strength enveloped him. For a moment, Andrew's body stiffened. *I'm supposed to be the strong one*, he thought. *I'm supposed to be the one who comforts—I'm the man.*

After a long moment, Andrew released the tension and sagged into Connor. He couldn't do it anymore, he realized. He couldn't pretend.

He had grown up with certain ideals from his dad, but he couldn't feign to be that strong.

Sometimes, he thought, *I just need someone to take care of me.*

Andrew tried not to sniffle in Connor's chest as he rested within Connor's strength. After a moment, he slowly reached up and wrapped his arms around Connor's waist. For a long moment, they embraced each other.

When Andrew released him, Connor stood back and looked at him. He brought his hands to Andrews's neck and rubbed away the tears running down his cheeks. He gave Andrew a reassuring smile, all the while holding his gaze.

"You give the best hugs," Andrew whispered.

"I learned at the Kitchen, and I try to pass them out as often as possible. Especially when someone is in need." Connor smiled. "The world could use a lot more hugs."

They stared at each other for a long moment, and Andrew could feel something fluttering through him. It was the strangest sensation he'd ever felt.

He was sad, and the weight of the world rested on him. A mountain that pressed him into the hard-packed earth. He'd felt as if he'd been struggling to breathe from the grip that the stress and anxiety held in his lungs. But when Connor hugged him—comforted and reassured him, the mountain was no longer as heavy.

"The world could also use a lot more of those sandwiches!" Connor joked before taking his seat and finishing the rest of his food. "Are you going to finish that?" he asked, at which Andrew pushed his plate across the counter.

"So, what is this Kitchen that Becky and you have mentioned?" Andrew asked as he started to clean up.

"A few years ago," Connor said between bites, "Becky and I ran into this kid at the park. It was early morning, and he looked hungry. He was sleeping under one of the large pine trees with a threadbare blanket."

"That's horrible."

"Yeah, it was unfortunate. Becky had just sold a painting, and I'd just received my first check from the pictures sold. So, we took the kid to a shelter to get something to eat, but they were out of food. The director told us that the funding for the kitchen portion had dried up. They had no choice but to move those funds to provide medical to those in need."

"We took one look at each other, and our eyes spoke what we already knew. So, we donated money and time to organize the efforts. We gathered others to volunteer, and we went to the college to petition them. Now they have a program that offers community hours to the Kitchen for their student work hours."

"Seriously? You did all that?" Andrew couldn't take his eyes off Connor. His heart flooded.

"We were young, but we knew that the money could not go with us if we suddenly died, so we decided to invest in the people who would be the next generation. It was a lot of hard work. We were going to school and working our daily jobs while also putting in the time to provide a safe place for those that didn't have one."

"And here I am whining and feeling sorry for myself about how horrible my life has been." Andrew shook his head in disappointment. "Going on about how I've been the victim in a relationship that I willingly stayed in when there are so many more important things in the world."

Connor squeezed his hand, pulling Andrews's eyes to his own. "I'm not a saint, and I don't want you to think this happened overnight. Becky and I were young and suddenly had more money than we'd ever had. Neither one of us grew up with a silver spoon."

"There were a lot of selfish parties, and we had plenty of fun before we accidentally stumbled on that kid in the park. We'd had too much to drink and ended up somewhere we shouldn't have been. Don't get me wrong, we had a good time that night, but that kid was our eye-opener. If we hadn't taken the path through the park, I honestly can't say that any of that would have ever happened."

"But you had that moment," Andrew said.

"I did, and it came when I was twenty-two. That was three years ago. Older than you are now."

"How do you know how old I am?" Andrew asks.

"I didn't, but Google knows everything. As does Facebook and the secret service men in my employ." Connor grinned at him, and they shared a laugh.

"So, is that what you wanted to do with this house?" Andrew asked.

Connor nodded, "Yeah, I wanted to keep this apartment for myself, and I wanted to make the basement and first two floors a home for kids who need a place to stay. Then, when I am completely done here, everything is set up, and I want to move, I will always have a place to stay when I come back or for whoever runs the house."

"I'd like to help!" Andrew said with a beaming smile. "I am getting my degree in business, and I was hoping to open a bakery one day."

"You bake?" Connor asked.

Andrew nodded. "What do you think my degree is in?"

"Cooking?"

"Baking and Pastries," Andrew corrected. "I'm a trained pastry chef, and I can cook."

"What the, why the hell are we eating egg croissants if we could be having cheese and raspberry Danishes?" Connor demanded, exasperated.

"Drizzled with glacé?"

"I'm officially in love." Connor smiled. Andrew looked at him wide-eyed. "With your cooking," Connor amended, then quickly stood and walked toward the bedroom.

The rest of the day was spent lying around the apartment, Connor walking the other three floors below and laying out his thoughts on what he'd like to see done with the space. The house was in decent shape, but you could tell whoever lived here before Connor purchased it had not taken care of it.

That afternoon, the smell of seasoned Italian meatballs filled the entire apartment, and Connor could not stop asking when they would be finished. Andrew laughed and finally pushed him toward the spare room. "Go work on building some of those muscles back up."

"Back up?" Connor's face opened in surprise. Eyebrows raised to the top of his forehead, eyes wide, and his lips pursed. "I'll show you what I need to build up." Laughing, he took three giant steps and grabbed Andrew's arm to tickle his side.

"Ahh!" The surprised laugh of shock tumbled from Andrews's mouth as he tried to jump aside but couldn't. Connor's grip was too tight, so he tried to grab the assaulting hand, but it was too fast and relentless.

"Uncle, uncle," he cried out between laughs and gasps for air.

The assaulting hand went around Andrew's waist and pulled him close. "That's what I thought." Connors's deep voice washed over Andrew like a wave on the shore. It wrapped around him like a protective cocoon he suddenly never wanted to leave.

Andrew couldn't tell what he was saying now. He was so focused on the strong arm wrapped around him and the fact that Connor smelled of soft pine in a summer breeze.

"Well?"

Shaking his head slightly and looking up into Connor's big eyes, he said, "I'm sorry, what?"

Connor's laugh was a rumble in his chest. His smile showed his perfect white teeth. "I asked if we should wash up before dinner. We've been exploring the dusty halls below, and maybe we should shower, eat, and then watch something before we have to get up for school tomorrow?"

"Sounds like a plan," Andrew said. He could already feel his penis pushing against Connor's thigh, painfully aware that they were going to get naked together again.

"Perfect," Connor purred and pulled him to the bathroom. He stripped down, then entered the shower and started the water. The steam condensed quickly in the cold room. "Come on." Connor beckoned him closer with a grin. "The cold is coming in!"

Andrew hastily undressed and stepped into the shower. All the shower heads were blasting at the same time, sending lukewarm water down their naked bodies.

Don't get hard; think of baseball—Jeremy in his baseball uniform—don't think about baseball! Andrew's mind wandered, and he fought to keep his eyes from straying down.

"Here." Connor had a soapy head. His eyes smiled as he squirted more shampoo into his hand and brought it to Andrew's head. His strong hands made quick work of it, and there were suds everywhere, tickling his forehead, getting into his ear, and running down Andrew's body.

Connor's strong fingers massaged the shampoo into his scalp. Andrew had never had his head washed by another guy. Only his grama had washed his hair—when he was little, she'd wash his head at the sink during the summer to cool him down.

The sensation of another man's strong hands caressing him sent shivers through his body. Andrew could feel the nerves overwhelm his common sense as his dick started to pulsate with the feelings he'd never experienced with someone else.

When Connor's hands disappeared, Andrew leaned back to wash the soap from his hair. Andrew could feel Connor's eyes on him like a hawk in the sky with the piercing gaze on the field mouse. Andrew's breath quickened along with his pulse. The warm water seemed to caress him as never before, and he was painfully—embarrassingly aware of how his body was reacting to the naughty thoughts that coursed through him.

Andrew opened his eyes just a fraction to see Connor through watery eyes. It was like he was watching through a waterfall as Connor stepped forward. His gaze was intent on the neck. His nerves tried to get him to move, to shy away, but it was like he was stuck in a dream and had no control over his body.

Connor slowly leaned in.

Nerves clutched at his stomach, and he didn't know what to do. This beautiful man was standing naked in front of him, and he just wanted to—Connor's full lips grazed Andrew's neck.

It was a quick movement, and it elicited the tiniest of gasps.

Andrew reached out as he started to fall backward, but Connor was quicker. His strong arms went around Andrew, pulling their wet bodies together. Their eyes stared into the other's. Breaths were quick, and that feeling of not knowing how the other man would respond was as thick as the steam in the shower.

"Drew," Connor whispered.

Andrew didn't know what to do. Actions and words blurred together in his mind, so he just stood stunned. The feelings that Connor invoked in him were something Cassie never had. *Oh, I wanted to fuck her plenty of times*, Andrew thought, but this feeling of lust, of need, a moment of weakness, or the most cogent step he would ever take elicited more feeling than Cassie—than anyone, ever had.

Another moment slipped by. Connor's strong, wet body was crushing against Andrew's. Andrew could feel that cock stirring against him. Maintaining eye contact, breath quickening, nerves electrifying his skin to prickle with anticipation, Andrew slowly shifted his head. Exposing the nape of his neck was all the answer Connor needed.

Connor's lips met Andrew's neck. Kiss after kiss before making his way up behind his ear and then to his jawline. Strong hands seemed to hold and grip everywhere. Andrew held on to Connor's arms and back, unable to prevent little gasps and moans from escaping him.

Andrew felt his cock thicken and rise in the steamy shower. He rose between Connor's legs as their lips met, all cohesive thought disappeared, and he was driven by action, by need, a want he'd never experienced . . .

He could feel Connor's balls resting atop his dick when Connor squeezed his legs tight, never missing a kiss.

Connor's strong hands slid down his back, cupping Andrew's tiny ass cheeks. Squeezing them before he pulled them apart, letting the warm water wash all over him.

Connor pulled Andrew forward and then released his ass. The tight squeeze his legs had on Andrew's cock sparked an electric feeling through his groin and his whole body in a way he'd never felt before.

"My hand could never do that," Andrew moaned, relishing the slide of Connor's dick against his stomach.

"No one has ever touched you?" Connor's deep voice was like thick, hot steam, everywhere. He stared down into Andrew's eyes; one hand took his neck as his thumb rubbed along Andrew's jaw while the other took hold of his ass and pulled him forward.

"Fuuck," Andrew studdered with a quiver running through his whole body, starting with his dick.

Taking hold of his hip, Connor started to push Andrew's hip away from him, then slammed him forward. "Uh, fuck," Andrew groaned as the electric feeling of the wet surface squeezing his cock became overwhelming.

His breath caught in his throat as his whole body seemed to transform. Before, he'd wandered around in a fog of insecurity and indecision, but when his body felt the sensations evoked by his cock, instinct took over. The cloudy sky of vacillation parted to allow the bright rays of lusty sunshine to brighten the world of sexual desire he'd always denied himself.

Andrew gripped Connor's muscular back as he started slowly thrusting before naturally increasing speed. Connor held him tight, eyes locked, watching each other as they verged on orgasm.

Small noises of ecstasy and desire escaped Andrew's throat, and compulsion took over his body. His fingers created marks as his grip slid from Connor's muscular wet back, and his thrusts became harder. His cock throbbed, and he could feel it enlarging as the pleasure almost painfully reached an apex. Connor's dick was rubbing against his stomach erotically, pushing him forward. They never broke eye contact.

"Oh, fuck." Andrew tried to pull away, but Connor held on to him and pulled him forward with rough hands.

Andrew's whole body tensed, and the heat from the steam was suddenly too much. His head grew light, his breath grew quicker, and Connor took control.

Connor took hold of Andrew and pulled his hips faster. Andrew threw his head back with a long groan as his orgasm wracked his whole body as cum erupted from him. Raking his nails down Connor's back, Andrew pulled back as far as he dared, then slammed forward again and again uncontrollably.

He pulled back again with a final thrust before collapsing against Connor.

Chest rising and falling quickly, Connor gave him a devious smirk. "That...was hot."

Andrew was at a loss for words as his dick gave a final twitch before starting to deflate.

"That"—Andrew tried to catch his breath—"was amazing."

"That was just the beginning." Connor leaned down to kiss those perfect lips when the timer in the kitchen suddenly went off.

Pulling away, Connor smiled. "Saved by the meat...balls."

They both laughed as they turned the shower off and dried themselves. Slipping into their briefs, they went to the kitchen and made their plates. Dinner was consumed in comfortable silence before they cleaned up and fell onto the couch.

Connor pulled Andrew on him, as they'd been when they woke up that morning.

"You smell like winter pine in the mountains," Andrew said as he inhaled Connor's chest.

"You smell like meatballs." Connor teased.

The room was dim, and neither was watching what was playing on the television. Andrew was relaxed against Connor's chest as Connor ran a finger lightly down his back.

"So, you have never?" Connor asked slowly.

"Nope, never."

"With anyone?"

"Nope, never."

"How did it feel?" Connor asked quietly.

"It...it was the most intense thing I have ever felt," Andrew answered. "At first, I didn't know what to do. I just tried to follow your lead, and then the feelings inside started to knot and twist, and this—this." Andrew shook his head against Connor's chest and grunted his feelings. "I can't even begin to describe it. This glorious feeling just grew and took over my whole being."

"Your body just knew."

"Oh, it knew, and it was begging for it. It wouldn't stop, and it would've taken it, if it had to!"

Connor laughed. "Is that so? Taken it?"

"Umm," Andrew said, then propped himself up, looking into Connor's eyes. "Is that what it is like?"

"What?"

"Sex?"

"No, that was just a little taste. A tease, if you will," Connor said. "The real thing is so much more intense.

"More intense?" Andrew asked in exasperated disbelief.

"With the right person, yes."

"I think, I think that I might have found that person," Andrew whispered into Connor's chest.

Chapter 5

"That cannot be comfortable." Her voice woke him up.

Bleary-eyed, Andrew picked himself up off Connor's chest and looked at Becky. They'd slept in the same position both nights, but the first night, they'd lain in the bed, and this night, on the oversized couch.

"What time is it?" Connor muttered, rubbing his strong hand down Andrew's back, giving a slight pat on the lower back.

"Seriously? Not even awake yet and, ugh, boys." She threw her hands up with a knowing chuckle. "I've coffee going, and speaking of, we need to be going, love."

Connor sat up, looking around. Sunlight streamed into the tall windows, and he knew he was late. "But I was so comfortable," he whined.

"Me too," Andrew said as he started to stand up.

"Again?" Becky gestured to the morning wood. "Seriously, that is impressive." She nodded with a hand motion towards Andrew's crotch before giving a silent clap accompanied by a mischievous grin.

"Bek!"

"Um, thanks?" Andrew wrapped the covers around him and went to the bathroom.

Dressed and caffeinated, the three of them left the apartment and went their respective ways. The next few days were a blur for everyone. Connor had work to do for the Kitchen when he was not working on his senior projects; Becky had needed time to look over artwork she was putting together for her show, and Andrew busied himself with his schoolwork while making small pastries for them to bring to the Kitchen.

Connor and Becky walked into the apartment late on Friday night to the smells of baked lasagna, roasted garlic bread, and a twinge of Caesar dressing.

"Seriously? I'm going to have to start working out with you if he keeps feeding us like this," Becky said as she patted her stomach.

"You're like ninety-eight pounds." Connor chuckled.

"I won't be for long if he feeds me more of this." She motioned to the table full of food. "I'm used to a glass of water and a smoke for lunch, and dinner is whatever I shove in my face as I'm running from one place to the next. And trust me, it is never anything you'd want to taste!"

She was sitting down already, placing a napkin on her lap.

"Well, you don't have to eat if you—"

"Shh." She held up a hand. "I cannot allow myself to be rude and turn down a table of food. If I were ever so ill-mannered, my grandmother would roll over in her grave."

They shared a laugh, and their meal before Andrew brought out a white-chocolate raspberry cheesecake with raspberry puree, grated white chocolate, and candied raspberries.

"Marry me?" Becky pleaded.

"Well, I was thinking about you today," Andrew said with a smile.

"What?" Becky and Connor said simultaneously. Then they looked at each other and laughed.

"You were talking about not knowing what to do for the third piece of the art show. You said you wanted to fill it with a canvas because the sculpture part was complete, as was the painting."

"Right?" Becky narrowed her eyes slightly.

"Well, I was thinking that, since you said you would like to do the human form, we could combine our two favorite things?" Andrew said hesitantly.

"And what is that?" Becky asked.

Andrew slid a piece of the cheesecake in front of them, took a sip of his white wine, and said, "Connor and dessert?"

"Yes."

"No." Connor shook his head.

Becky glared at Connor as she slowly lifted the fork to her mouth.

"You're the perfect male form," Becky replied.

"You know how I feel about exploiting my body for money," Connor said.

"You weren't exploited, love." Becky dropped the fork back to the plate and then met his gaze. "You willingly took those pictures."

"They were sold without my permission—"

"And you made a lot of money off of them, and you could again, honey," Becky reached over and took Connor's hand. "You could use what we 'normal folks' don't have to enhance the world."

"By selling my body like a prostitute?"

"By selling pictures that I have created from the inspiration of your natural beauty given to you by the grace of your momma's loins."

Connor gave a hard, painful squeeze of Becky's hand. "No, and that's final."

"Con—"

"Wait, hear me out," Andrew said. "If the item sells, we could do something on a grander scale, like, I dunno, make a calendar. Everyone needs a calendar."

"That's a great idea!"

"That's a horrible idea!"

"And the proceeds from the calendar sales could go to finishing the house."

Both Becky and Connor stared at Andrew for a long moment.

"He's got a point," Becky said. "And we will rock those pastries if they taste like this!" She took another bite of the dessert, making little whimpering noises.

"Drew," Connor said with all seriousness, "I have never tasted anything like this! Oh. My. God!"

Andrew could feel his face flush.

"Seriously, how did you do this? It's like creamy and tart with a chocolaty—"

"Back off, Bek, I saw him first." Connor laughed.

"I don't kink shame, but I'm pretty sure you could use this for food sex, and anyone would be into it!"

"Bek!"

"Oh Lord." Andrew snickered, then took a hesitant drink of his wine.

"Ugh, I am stuffed to the gills!" Becky leaned back, rubbed her stomach, and unbuttoned her pants.

They shared two or three more glasses of wine as they joked around about the upcoming Halloween event being held in the quad next month and the art show Becky was putting together. They left any serious talk under the table and just enjoyed the evening. It was getting late, so the three of them cleaned the kitchen, put the food away, and then Becky went home.

"What now?" Connor asked, stretching his arms as high as he could. "Want to watch some TV? Or we could—"

"Shower?" Andrew asked.

"Umm, now that's an idea!" Connor drawled, tapping his finger to his chin with a mischievous grin. Dropping his hands, he called out, "Last one in has to wash the other first," and took off toward the bedroom door.

"What!?" Stunned, Andrew gave chase quickly. He was smaller and faster, but Connor had the head start.

Peals of laughter rang out as Connor raced across the bedroom, and Andrew jump-tackled him onto the bed. They tumbled down, guffawing, then rolled off the bed to the floor. As they untangled themselves, Connor tickled Andrew, who shrieked in surprise.

Back on his feet, Connor was through the door and naked by the shower by the time Andrew picked himself up off the floor.

"You lose!"

"But did I?" Andrew smiled and rubbed his hands together conspiratorially. "Did I really?"

"Umm, yep!" Connor laughed, stepped into the shower, and turned on all the heads.

Andrew followed him into the steamy shower. "We've got to stop meeting like this, sir," he said, reaching for the soap and loofah.

"Well, if you insist—"

"Get back here, mister." Andrew pulled Connor away from the shower door and planted the soapy loofah into the middle of his muscular chest.

Starting on the other man's chest and arms, he worked his way lower until he was kneeling directly before Connor's penis. It was thick and starting to awaken as it lay against his heavy balls. Gently he began to soap Connor's crotch and then worked the loofah across the front of his cock and balls as if he were petting them.

"Umm, if you want them clean, you might have to go in a little more," Connor suggested playfully, his dick rising to the occasion.

"Oh?" Andrew bit his bottom lip.

Reaching out, he slowly wrapped his hand around Connor's dick; it quivered in response to his touch. "Yeah?" he asked.

Connor moaned. "Mmm, yeah," he agreed, gazing down at Andrew as he knelt before him. His eyes grew hazy with pleasure.

Andrew studied the dick in his hand. He'd touched his own before, obviously; many, many, many more times than he cared to count. But he'd never once touched another man's dick. Not even that time with Jermey on the beach or the one or two times he'd jerked off with a teammate in the shower after sports practice.

His cock was hard, but it also felt surprisingly soft—as if there were a cushy wrap around a steel rod below. It was not something he'd ever taken the time time to explore with his own cock. Usually, that had been a quickie of rubbing one out for pleasure before going about the day. With Connor, he slowly moved his hand back and forth, exploring the feel of another man in his hand, which elicited groans from Connor. Touching someone else was different, but he loved the way he was making Connor feel.

This large Greek god of a man was suddenly putty in his hands, and with that thought, he started massaging his balls. They hung low and heavy as he played with them. He gave them a slight tug, which brought an "Uh, careful," whisper from above.

As he continued playing with Connor's balls, Andrew slipped one hand between his legs, gently pushing them apart so his fingers could tease Connor's hole while he began to massage his frenulum with the thumb of his other hand. Connor reached out to hold on to the wall and started to move his hips to the rhythm of Andrew's hand around his penis.

Andrew leaned in and swiped the tip of the dick he was holding with his tongue. The salty taste was evident, and it sort of tasted like his own. Who hadn't tried their own jizz once or twice? Gently, he licked around the head for a moment before finally taking it into his mouth.

"Oh, fuck," Connor moaned. One large, strong hand took him by the back of the head as Connor's hips continued to hump further into Andrew's mouth, who suddenly felt his gag reflex kick in.

He struggled to breathe through his nose and tried to pull off Connor's dick, but Connor was in the moment. Then Andrew started to gag.

"Oh, fuck." Connor pulled his cock from Andrew's mouth. "You okay?" he asked, going to his knees as Andrew bent over, trying not to vomit as he started to dry heave.

"Drew, you okay? I'm so sorry," Connor rubbed his back for a moment.

"Sorry," Andrew choked out.

"No, no, don't be. I'm sorry I got carried away. I know it can be a mouthful."

"My first time," Andrew said, tears streaming down his eyes.

"Your first?" Connor asked, and Andrew nodded in confirmation. "You've never done this before?"

"No."

"Have you ever had a blowjob yourself?" Connor asked.

"No." Andrew put his head down in embarrassment. He knew this would be difficult since he was a virgin who'd never had sex with anyone and never messed around at all except that one night with Jeremy. Even with Cassie, it had only been some making out since she wanted to wait until she was married—he'd never seen her fully nude.

"When you said virgin, you meant, like, one hundred percent never touched another dick virgin. Never gave oral or—"

"Never." Andrew shook his head in defeat.

Connor took him by the chin and raised his head. "I'm sorry I was rough. I'll make sure that it never happens again."

Andrew stared into those gorgeous gray eyes, knowing Connor spoke the truth.

Connor helped Andrew to his feet, and they quickly finished washing, then shut down the shower and started to dry themselves off. They made their way to the bed and climbed in.

"I was thinking," Connor said as he started moving closer to Andrew, "we could just keep this arrangement like it is." He sounded unsure.

"What do you mean?"

"Well, I was thinking that we could just bunk together instead of adding another bed. With the other room set up, this kinda feels comfortable and, and I don't know. It just feels right."

"Kinda comfortable?" Andrew laughed. "If you consider waking up with me stretched out on you like Cleopatra on a chaise comfortable." He smiled warmly.

Connor slowly moved his hand across the comforter until their pinkies barely grazed each other. It almost felt as if electricity was sparking between them.

"But I do think that is comfortable," Connor said, low and slow. Then he glanced at Andrew out of the corner of his eye.

Andrew averted his gaze, suddenly shy. "I've never been in any type of relationship with another guy."

"Have you been in a relationship with anyone other than her?"

"No."

"Did it hurt?" Connor asked.

"Did what hurt?"

"The first time we showered."

"No, it didn't hurt," Andrew said.

Connor glanced at Andrew. "If it feels right, don't be afraid to follow it. It might not be the norm that you are used to, but just trust in yourself, and it won't lead you astray." Connor's voice was low and sincere. I won't lead you astray, Andrew."

"I think that was the first time you used my full name."

"I figured she called you Andrew, so I would have something that was just you and me?" Connor glanced down for a moment, then met Andrew's eyes.

Andrew smiled. "I like it," he said quietly, pulling a smile from Connor.

After a long moment of comfortable silence, Andrew confessed, "I, well, there was this one time with my best friend's brother." He paused.

Connor rubbed their pinkies together and started to move his hand over Andrew's. It was as if he could sense that this was hard, and wanted to protect him from whatever would come.

"We had snuck out, the three of us, when camping. Their dad woke, so my friend Sean went back, but his brother and I stayed behind. Suddenly, he started kissing me, and I kissed him back. We even began to rub against each other."

"You were fooling around?"

"Horsing around more like. We were in camp and decided to head to the river to go skinny dipping. Then we started to wrestle in the water, and the next thing I know, I'm kissing him on the beach."

"Huh." Connor smiled. "Was it any good?"

"The kissing?"

"Yeah, the kissing!"

"It was my first time ever. It was awkward at first, but then it just felt...right."

"Like, did you bump your teeth awkwardly?" Connor shuddered.

"Ew, no!"

Connor laughed, "Yeah, that's not the best way to start or finish a kiss. Have you ever bit down on aluminum foil?"

"Ouch!" Andrew put his hand to his mouth.

"Exactly how that feels, and seriously, you never forget it." He snickered. "Go on."

"We started rubbing ourselves against each other, and that's how his dad found us."

"Seriously?" Connor looked horrified. "He caught you making out?"

"To my everlasting shame." Andrew looked everywhere but at Connor.

A long moment of silence passed as Connor gave him space to gather his thoughts and continue his story. "What happened?"

"Well, we packed camp that night and went home. We arrived first thing in the morning, and he made Sean and Jeremy go inside while he had a 'talk' with me," Andrew air-quoted. "He told me that I was never to step foot in his house or talk to or interact with either of his kids. He threatened to call his priest and tell my parents. I stood there, ashamed of everything, and wished the ground would open up and swallow me whole."

Andrew took a deep breath. "Eventually, they moved."

Connor rolled onto his side and looked Andrew in the eye, "Well, I will never hurt you like she did, and I will never shame you as he did. I know this is all new, and I'm more than willing to take it a day at a time. If you want to take it a day at a time with me, that is."

They lay staring deep into each other's eyes. Andrew could see how open and honest Connor was and knew that he'd always been that way and always would be. Something inside was drawing him to Connor and had been since the moment the volleyball knocked his ass out.

"Okay," Andrew whispered.

"Okay?" Connor asked. Reaching over, he took Andrew gently by the neck, rubbing his jawline with his thumb before leaning in and gently kissing him.

Chapter 6

Jogging through the park, Andrew kept pushing until he started to fall behind. *What in the Sam Hell was I thinking?* he asked himself for the thousandth time in the last hour. He'd agreed to start working out with Connor, but only if Connor would learn how to cook with him. At first, the arrangement had been amicable. They'd completed some in-house workouts and made some easy three-ingredient desserts from a Baking with Kids cookbook.

Andrew slowed but just enough to watch Connor stroll through the park in the chilly air of an early fall morning. He admired his long gait, his muscles as they contracted, his elbows and shoulders pumped to and fro with each stride, and the sweaty shirt that clung to his bulging back muscles.

Realizing his shorty running shorts were getting a little tight; he tried to push those thoughts aside. That was until Connor's pace faltered; he twisted around and started running backward. Watching Connor's pecs bounce in the same rhythm as his cock suddenly had Andrew's heart rate up and breathing at a whole new speed.

They started to jog back home but walked the last three blocks. Connor was big on explaining what they were doing, but then Andrew was the same way when they were in the kitchen.

When they'd reached the third story of the house, Connor had them stretching. Andrew spread his legs, bent at the hips, and placed his palms on the floor as Connor stood behind him, helping him get into position.

Connor's strong hands were thorough in their relentless push and pull to help Andrew get into the correct stretching positions. The entire time Connor's cock pressed into Andrew's ass.

"A steamy hot shower will help relax the muscles after such extraneous exercise. Well, cardio."

"Uh-huh." Andrew sounded as if he was trying to stretch his legs and waist simultaneously. At this moment, breathing was the best he could do.

Connor patted him on the back. "okay, champ, time to hit the showers," he said, doing a bad impression of a coach.

Andrew stood and stretched his hip briefly, then yelled, "Last one in washes the other first," as he raced across the apartment.

Peals of laughter rang out, and clothes were flung all around as they tried to beat each other to the shower. Andrew stretched out his arm toward the shower right when Connor reached around him with his long arms to touch it first.

"Not fair!" Andrew laughed as he tried to catch his breath.

Connor grinned as he pushed Andrew into the shower. "Poor sport, hum?" he teased as he took hold of Andrew's shirt and pulled it off in one swift motion.

"Am not!" Andrew stuck out his bottom lip, which quickly turned into a smile as the shower heads flared to life full blast.

Steam quickly filled the walk-in shower, fogging up the glass and the room's mirrors beyond.

Connor acted like he was doing the breaststroke through the overwhelming amount of steam. "Loofah, I'll never let you go!"

"Oh, hush!" Andrew said teasingly. "Or I'll let you drown."

Stepping up to Andrew, Connor gently washed his chest and arms, making large eyes at him and giving him a lopsided smile.

"Oh yeah?" Andrew asked with a smile. "You think so?"

"Uh-huh." Connor's cock suddenly twitched and started rising.

"You're incorrigible!"

Connor soaped his stomach and arms, but then his hands suddenly took hold of Andrew's dick. "That is seriously big!"

"Think so?" A smirk crossed Andrew's face.

"Love a hot little twink with a huge dick." Connor soaped up his hands and ran them along Andrew's cock and balls.

"Twink?" Andrew raised his eyebrows.

"It's a thing. Like, a body type in gay terms," Connor said, but his sole focus was on the growing dick in his soapy hands. "Otter, bear, daddy, and whatever else they say nowadays that I'm not on the up and up about." Connor glanced up and smiled his wicked little grin before his eyes returned to the task in hand.

Leaning his head back with a groan, Andrew waited for him to go to his knees. He was anticipating the feeling of his cock in Connor's mouth. The very thought made him twitch in eagerness.

Connor took him by the shoulders and turned him around. The hot water ran down his back as the loofah crossed his thin shoulders and then down to the top of his crack. Gently, Connor pushed the loofah lower, eliciting a small grunt from Andrew.

"Sorry," he whispered in Andrew's ear. "Here, this is better." Wet, soapy fingers slid through his ass cheeks, rubbing up and down before a finger slid against his hole.

An involuntary groan escaped Andrew, and he pushed his ass out slightly to embrace this new feeling.

A strong hand pushed against the middle of his back, pressing his chest into the cold tile. Rough hands pulled his hips back before spreading his pert little cheeks wide, exposing his intimate parts. Andrew's hot breath fogged the cold tiles in nervous anticipation. His breath quickened with his pulse, and he turned his head to look over his should when he felt Connor rub his stubbled cheek along his smooth ass.

The sensation took his breath away. Connor pulled his cheeks apart and pushed his face in. His tongue flicked and circled his hole in constant motion, and a groan escaped him. Strong hands kneaded his cheeks, then pulled them open before squeezing them shut against stubbled cheeks.

"Oh, fuuck," Andrew moaned and pushed back against Connor's mouth.

Pulling away, Connor glanced up and gave one cheek an open palm smack that resonated throughout the shower. "Yeah?"

In answer, Andrew reached back, taking Connor by the hair and pushing his face back into him.

"Oh fuck, oh Connor," he whimpered.

Connor reached through Andrew's legs and took hold of his straining cock. Andrew started to reach down, but Connor pushed his hand away as he began at the base and pulled his cock long and tight, all the while pushing into Andrew's ass with his tongue.

Groans echoed through the bathroom as Connor started jerking his cock faster. Another open palm to the cheek, and Andrew pushed back until Connor's tongue was inside him. Connor grabbed Andrew's hip to hold him from bucking off his tongue as he jacked him faster.

"Cumming!" Andrew yelled into the tile as jizz exploded from the tip of his cock. Spurt after spurt, Andrew clawed at the tile in total ecstasy.

After his final shot, Andrew twitched to the side. "Um, sensitive!" His voice all but cracked.

Connor ran his strong hands up Andrew's back, taking him by the shoulders and massaging the tense muscles. Andrew melted into Connor when he wrapped his muscular arms around him.

Laying his head back on Connor's shoulder, he whispered, "That was amazing."

Making their way to the bed, they claimed their usual places, with Connor on his back and Andrew draped over him like a second sheet. Connor ran his fingertips across Andrew's back, which was building up definition thanks to their workouts and healthy diet. They chatted about their day and what the near future held for them, such as the upcoming Halloween bash, before both drifted off to sleep.

Connor was floating in the bed with the cold sheets draped all around him. He reached out, and his hands took hold of a warm body. He pulled it close. Lips met his, and a solid need to consume the lust within took hold. Small groans escaped them when he felt that perfect little ass sitting on him.

His cock jumped as it slid between those skinny little cheeks, and the tip of his dick pushed into those low-hanging balls. The friction started to grow as those hips slid the length of his cock and back faster and faster.

"Oh, fuck," he muttered as his eyes fluttered open to see Andrew with his mouth around his cock. His arms were stretched out, and his fist gathered mounds of comforter in his pleasure. Another look back down at those full lips wrapped around his engorged cock pushed him over the edge.

"Drew?" Connor moaned as his hip bucked involuntarily. "Oh fuck, I'm gonna cum," he grunted.

Andrew pulled off the tip, but his tongue expertly tickled all around the head, and then his lips wrapped around Connor's shaft as jizz shot from him. The first shot landed on his pillow and across his cheek and the next in his mouth, but before he could move, the third hit his chin and his chest.

Andrew started to slow in his administrations to Connor's cock, then gave him an appraising look. "I've never seen anyone cum so much. No, seriously, I don't think a porn star has you beat in baby batter making."

"That was amazing." Connor relaxed into the bed, his eyes fluttered closed, his breath slowing. He could feel himself drifting off after watching Drew's lips around him.

"Connor." Andrew laughed. "You can't go back to sleep."

"Why not?" he muttered.

"We were going to the Kitchen."

"Fuck," Connor groaned. "But I don't wanna." He slapped at the bedding.

"Besides, you've got a mess to clean up." Andrew laughed up until the point that Connor grabbed him and pulled him onto his chest. The cum spread between them in a warm, sticky goo.

"I hate you."

"Aw, now! I thought you loved me." Connor rubbed his back with a mischievous giggle, and then he leaned in and kissed Andrew on the forehead, smearing more cum on him.

"I'll start the shower," Andrew said, jumping from the bed and wiggling his hips.

"Mmm, you little minx." Connor climbed from the bed, trying to catch the cum running down his chest so not to drip on the carpet.

Washed, dried, and dressed, the two went to the cobblestone street down by the flood wall. The Mississippi ran just on the other side, and it was known to flood, so the wall had been built to help protect the town. They had also allowed local artists to paint the wall so it didn't look too prison-like.

The building Connor led them to was an unassuming place that looked out on the graffiti, which gave the view a colorful disposition. When they walked in, a tiny bell above the door went off.

"That's to let us know when someone comes in—"

"You don't say!" Andrew's pretend shocked face made Connor smile.

"When it's not busy, smart-ass," Connor laughed. "When it's busy, and we are serving, we raise the bell. But we don't want to be in the back and be caught unawares when someone comes in on us."

"Hey, bro!" a voice called out as a yellow blur sped past Andrew, wrapping arms around Connor, twirling him around, and trying to pick him up with little success.

"So, Andrew, I want you to meet Aiyden." Connor grinned as he hugged the boy in a yellow shirt. A beaming face smiled up at Andrew, and he could see the admiration for Connor in those dark eyes. "This is my brother from another mother."

"So, you're him, huh? Andrew?" Aiyden made a *whoo-whoo* sound as he wiggled his eyebrows.

"Bro!" Connor tapped the back of his head. "You're supposed to be playing it cool!" And he gave Ayden two winks.

"Aw, you know I'm messing with you." Aiyden pushed Connor away, looked Andrew up and down, and then walked away, saying, "Not bad, bro."

"Oh Lord, give me the strength," Connor said with a smirk. Then, he took Andrew by the hand, leading them into the back. "Aiyden was the boy we found that night. He's the reason all of this exists," Connor explained as he walked into the open kitchen in the back.

"This is huge!" Andrew said, looking wide-eyed at the state-of-the-art kitchen he had not expected.

"That's what I said," Becky called out, bringing laughs from everyone in the place.

"This is where the magic happens." Connor ignored her.

"That's also what I say!!" Becky laughed.

"Good one!" This came from Aiyden as he jumped up on one of the stainless tables.

"Seriously? I thought you two were on my side."

"Oh honey, don't let them rattle your snake," a little unassuming old woman said as she wiped her hands on a dry towel. Her smile brought a plethora of wrinkles that spoke of years of smiles and brought a smile from Andrew as well. "That's what he's for!"

She pointed at Andrew and then cackled like the wicked stepmother.

"Et tu, Alma?" Connor put a hand over his heart with a pained look. "Et tu?"

"Oh, now, sonny, we are just having a little go at it—"

"So is he," Aiyden shouted, and they all laughed.

"That's it, we're leaving!" Connor smiled, taking hold of Andrew's hand and turning toward the door.

"You know we only tease because we care!" Alma threw her towel at Connor.

"You know we love you more than, well," Aiyden looked around at everyone. " Well, you know we love you."

Insert an award-winning smile for his bro, and an exaggerated wink.

Andrew laughed.

"Incorrigible!" Connor muttered with an eye roll. "Well, anyway, everyone, this is Andrew, and Andrew, this is everyone," he said, waving a palm at all of them.

"Sounds like all of you will get along just fine. Laugh at me, huh?" Connor pulled Andrew's arm up and tickled his side.

Andrew yelped and jumped back from the wiggling fingers.

"Save it."

"Get a room."

"I'm gonna be sick,"

"At least you all agree on one thing!" Connor snickered and led Andrew into the kitchen, showing him where all the food was prepped and prepared, including the four convection ovens, four large kettles, and the hot holds.

"This is very impressive!" Andrew gazed around in awe. "Seriously, this is a full commercial kitchen. How did you do all this?"

"Well." Becky slid up to them, taking Andrew by the arm. "You see, our boy Connor here—"

"Bek…" Connor took Andrew's arm back. "We don't need to go into all of that right now. Really, I just wanted to show him and see if he wanted to help us prepare for the meal tonight?"

"I'd love to!" Andrew smiled, and it touched his eyes.

"Perfect. I'll show you where and what's on the menu!" Becky said, pulling Andrew along.

They worked for four hours making the soup, baked chicken in lemon sauce with redskin potatoes and green beans. Andrew worked on an éclair cake that he'd decided to throw together at the last moment, hoping it would set in time.

During their time in the Kitchen, Connor often paused what he was doing and watched Andrew. How he interacted with the team, and how they interacted with him. He watched with that smile that pulled his left cheek up just so and that open-mouthed laugh when a dirty joke popped from someone unexpectedly.

"Oh honey, you have it bad!" Alma patted him on the back.

Chapter 7

Becky walked into the apartment, yelling, "Are you ready? We are going to be more than fashionably late!"

"Yeah, yeah." Connor laughed as he walked from the bedroom in a red outfit complete with red paint smeared under his eyes and a red bowl helmet.

"What the fuck are you? A red dildo?"

Andrew laughed from his place at the kitchen counter as he watched the interaction. He'd been anticipating Becky's smartass comments on Connor's costume. Her sarcasm was unrivaled.

Andrew's laughter pulled Becky's attention to him. She gave him a quick once over before clapping her hands over her mouth. Andrew sat on the counter in white pants and shirt with black dots all over him.

"No, the fuck you didn't!" Becky burst into laughter, clapping one hand over her mouth and bringing an arm across her stomach.

"You're a Dalmatian and fire hydrant?"

"I thought it ingenious!" Connor looked at Andrew for support.

"We don't have time to change, but if people think you're into watersports, I haven't the foggiest idea where they'd get that from."

She turned and walked from the apartment.

"Yeah, well, people aren't going to have the *foggiest* idea who you are!" Connor called after her.

A resounding, "Will too," echoed up the staircase.

They left the apartment and headed for the quad. The Halloween party started at three, with the main festivities consisting of games and contests. The party would then move to the rec center with a corn maze, dance, and costume contest.

It was almost five, and the quad was filled with college kids milling about. The brisk October air would soon be much colder as the sun would soon be setting, which is when the party would move across campus.

They met up with some friends from Becky's art class. One of them, Joanne, was dressed as Dora and asked, "And what are you supposed to be? A blast from the past?"

"See!" Connor shouted a little too loudly.

"I'm 80s Madonna." Becky put her hand on her hips, posing as if she were in front of the paparazzi on the red carpet.

"Who?" A guy standing next to Joanne gave Connor and Andrew a questioning look, then shrugged.

"Seriously, Joannie? Whose baby is this?" Becky asked.

"You wanted to know." Connor chuckled as Andrew stage-whispered towards the new guy, "I didn't know either."

"How can you not know? She is one of the greatest singers of all time!" Becky was now in defense mode.

"To you!" Joanne said, shaking her head.

"To them"—Connor pointed to Andrew and Jack—"she's someone who is played on the *Oldies* station that they don't listen to."

"What has this world come to?" Becky shook her head in mock despair.

"Now that we have that settled," Joanne said, exaggerating and rolling her eyes, "everyone, this is Jack. He is in the Intro to Art that I teach for credit. He's a newbie here. Jack, these are my friends."

"Nice to meet you," Andrew held out his hand.

"Pleasure is all mine." Jack took Andrew's hand and kissed it.

"Oh, um…" Andrew stammered, and the blush of red quickly started up his neck and into his cheeks.

"I'm Connor," Connor quickly butted in and pulled Andrew's hand from those lips. Andrew glanced at Connor, saw what could only be described as jealousy staring back at him, and smiled.

"Nice to meet you." Jack gave him a curt nod before dismissing Connor when a hot, young guy walked by.

"He's a little forward, sorry," Joanne said, slapping his shoulder. "And needs to learn manners or etiquette or something."

"I'm Becky." Their friend held out her hand, and Jack took it with a, "Pleasure to meet you."

Connor rolled his eyes.

"How about we go sign up for the contest, Jack? Whom are you supposed to be?" Becky took him by the arm as he started to turn toward Andrew again.

"Jack from Jack and the Beanstalk."

"How clever," Becky said, turning them toward the far end of the quad.

"Sorry about him," Joanne said as she followed Becky. "He's a young'un." She grinned mischievously. "Soo, Connor, I didn't know you were into watersports—"

"Seriously?"

"Told you so!!" Becky called over her shoulder, and Andrew laughed loudly.

"Yeah, I'd have gone with a fireman and a Dalmatian." Joanne patted him on the arm.

"Bestiality, what?" Becky looked at them with a shocked expression.

"What is wrong with you?" Joanne laughed.

"A lot!" Connor said, shooting her a look. "How much time do you have?" He smiled at Joanne, and they all walked into the crowd together.

The party moved from the quad to the rec and bled late into the night. The music was deafening.

"Want to get out of here?" Connor squeezed Andrew's hand.

"Sure," Andrew smiled. The smile he reserved for Connor when he looked at him. The one that moved to his eyes and made them twinkle. The one Connor would catch on his face when watching from across the room.

He melts my heart!

"Cool, let me tell Becky—"

A girl dressed entirely in black stumbled into Andrew, knocking him to the ground. He went down with a surprised yelp, and whoever she was stumbled a few feet away, then turned back to them.

"Did you have to body-check him?" Connor asked as he helped Andrew to his feet. "You okay?"

"AHH, you've got to be fucking kidding me!" the girl yelled in a drunken slur. "I always knew you were a spineless mutt!"

"What the—"

"You left me for him?"

"Cassie?" Andrew's surprise was written all over his face. His ex was dressed in black, with a witch's hat and green smeared across her face as if she was painted for war.

She wobbled on her feet. "You just disappeared from the float, and I never heard from you! Come home, and all your shit is gone?" her voice was rising, and people started to give them space and murmur.

"That's enough," Connor said, standing in front of him. "You're drunk and need to—"

"Don't talk to me, man stealer!" Cassie yelled.

"He didn't steal me, Cass." Andrew found his voice and stepped around Connor. "He's shown me what it is like to be wanted, but more importantly, he's shown me what it is like to be respected."

"Wanted? Respected? A sniveling dog of a man? Who'd respect that?" She cackled as if getting into the character she wore.

A guy appeared on the crowd's edge, dressed as a sexy monkey, as if that were even possible, with little feathery wings from his back. "Hey, Cass, let 'em be. How about—"

"Shut up." She waved him off as if shooing away a fly.

"That's how a woman treats a man who doesn't have a spine to stand up for himself. Just like you and all the other mutts around here that need a strong woman to take charge."

"Come on." Connor started to pull Andrew away.

"Have you told your parents?" Cassie suddenly shouted. "Have you told them you're queer?"

"Andrew." Connor tried to pull him into the crowd now giving them plenty of space, watching the drama unfold.

"Bible-loving, closed-minded parents? How do you think they'll take it?"

"Just like I have," Andrew said. "One day at a time. And I know that they'll appreciate the way Connor treats me, which is better than you ever did. Even if he does have a dick."

The crowd cheers.

"You fucking fa—"

"Finish that sentence, and I'll show you equality, bitch." Becky stepped from the crowd.

"Who're you?"

"The one who's gonna beat your ass back to Oz." Becky took a threatening step forward.

"And I'm right behind her." A muscular woman dressed as She-Hulk stepped up behind Becky.

"And me," another said from the other side of the circle.

A chorus of "And me!" started to come from all directions.

"You leave 'em be!"

"He's better off without a ho like you!"

"Get on your monkey and fly away, bitch!"

Cassie looked all around the circle in a drunken daze. The disbelief that they would not back her and her narrow-minded views of the world emanated off her.

"Fuck all of you!" she screamed at the top of her lungs. "Curt!"

The good-looking, muscular monkey man stepped into the circle. His face was one of anger but, most of all, of hurt.

"Get me out of here—"

"You're a strong woman. Get yourself out of here!" he said. "I'm not your bitch!" Then he disappeared into the throng of people.

The crowd went wild.

Four campus police suddenly entered the drama circle and tried to get Cassie to come with them. She screamed, *"Don't touch me!!"* and shoved one of the officers. Two others stepped up, taking her by the arms, and they dragged her along as another officer led the way through the crowd, and the one she'd pushed brought up the rear.

The drama circle dissipated with the loss of Cassie fueling the flames.

Becky walked over and put a hand on their shoulders. "I've got your back. Now and always." She gave Andrew and Connor a sad smile.

Connor looked down at Andrew, whose head had lowered in shame. "She's right," he whispered.

"What?" Connor asked.

"She's right." He looked up as the tears rolled down. "My parents are very conservative in their thinking, and I don't know how they will accept an alternative lifestyle."

"Seriously?" Becky asked.

Andrew nodded, and his shoulders slumped.

"Look." Jack was suddenly standing beside them as if he'd just appeared from thin air. "My parents are the most conservative people you've ever met. I feared they would reject me, and I was heartbroken to even tell them. You don't have to announce yourself to the world like some debutant presented to the queen in 1847."

"How'd they take it?" Andrew asked.

"It took them a minute, and my mom cried a lot, but she talked with my dad . . . okay, so it took more than a minute." Jack grimaced. "But in the end, they came around. I'm their son! How could they not, right?" Jack smiled and framed his face with his hands while batting his eyelashes at them.

Connor took Andrew's chin in his hand and lifted his face. His heart quickly beat with anger at the fact that this had happened. His Drew was hurt, and he hadn't done more to protect him.

"I'll always be here for you," Connor told him. "No matter what. If you don't ever tell them, that's okay. If you tell them tomorrow, that's okay. We no longer have to live by anyone else's rules."

Connor's eyes became hard like a stone in their conviction to protect Andrew. They were bearing into Andrew's soul to let him know how true those words were for him.

"We live by our own rules." Connor wiped the tears from Andrew's cheeks, smearing the white and black makeup even more, making him look like a Salvador Dali painting.

Then he crushed their lips together.

A few catcalls and a *Get a room!* from the crowd brought a smile to both of them, and they broke off their kiss.

"Let's get you home and showered?"

"It's like you've read my mind," Andrew said with a nervous chuckle as if he were trying to shake off the drama of the night.

"Besides…" Andrew visibly shook himself. "This isn't how I wanted my birthday to end."

"What?" Connor and Becky blurted at the same time.

"Today's your birthday?"

"How did I not know that?" Connor asked, flabbergasted.

"We've never really talked about it." Andrew shrugged. "It's not that important—"

"Everything about you is important!" Connor pulled him into the crowd, setting off toward home.

Becky side-eyed Jack, who looked at her innocently. "Really?"

"What, really?"

"They came around?"

"Fuck no, they disowned me in a heartbeat. I told them the night before I moved to college. They told me it was the last night I'd ever stay in their house and to take whatever I didn't want burned. Since I was going to burn in hell."

Becky wrapped her arm around him. "You've got us, kid."

"Thanks." His sad smile made a brief appearance before he twisted it into a more cheerful one, suppressing his sadness. "I think we need a witch hunt!" He laughed and then started dancing off into the crowd.

Connor brought Andrew home and had him in the shower within moments of entering the door. The two washed each other and removed their makeup before the kissing began.

"I'm so sorry," Connor whispered as he pulled off Andrew's lips. Caressing that beautiful face with his thumb and staring deeply into his eyes.

"When's your birthday?" Connor asked.

"January," Connor said. "Worst birthday month ever!"

"Really? Why?"

"No one ever comes to your party because it is cold, snowing or ice has covered the world, and they can't get out. Also, all the money has been spent on Christmas and taxes, so gifts are minimal. And they are always wrapped in Christmas paper."

"You've given this a lot of thought," Andrew said.

"Twenty-five years of thought."

"Twenty-five-old-man years," Andrew said teasingly.

"Take that back." Connor wrapped a strong arm around Andrew, pulling them together. "Or I'll show you an *old man*." His lip pulled up to the right in his mischievous way.

"I'm counting on it," Andrew whispered as they kissed.

Hands slid and groped as the sounds of kissing and moans of desire echoed off the tile. Soon, the shower heads started to turn cold, and they exited the shower and dried each other off. Connor led Andrew to the bed, laid him on his back, and gently lowered himself on top of him.

They kissed as they rubbed their hard cocks between them. The friction started sending waves of pleasure through Andrew, and his breathing began to increase.

"Um, not yet." Connor smiled, pulling their grinding cocks apart, which elicited a disappointed groan from Andrew. "There's so much more fun to be had for the birthday boy!"

Connor kissed those swollen lips, then worked his way down to Andrew's chest before attacking each nipple with small nibbles and flicks of his tongue. His strong hands caressed the smooth skin along Andrew's side before reaching his groin, where he cupped those low-hanging smooth balls that rested between his legs.

"Mmm, they feel full." Connor looked up at him with hooded eyes as he gently separated those smooth legs and dragged his chin down Andrew's chest to his belly button. He made a brief stop as he circled his innie with his tongue before continuing to that massively large, throbbing cock.

He rubbed his stubbly chin across Andrew's cock, then kissed the tip before flicking his tongue against the head.

"Ugh, tease." Andrew giggled, and his only response was that mischievous smile.

Running his tongue down the shaft as it jumped in anticipation of what was to come next, Connor sank down to those full balls. Gently, he pushed his nose against Andrew's leg and smelled the soapy musk of man, then he flicked his tongue against the skin, bringing forth moans of delight.

One by one, he pulled each testicle into his mouth. Gently sucking and massaging them with his tongue as his large hands ran up and down those smooth thighs. After bathing his balls, Connor slowly started to move further down until his chest lay on the mattress and his ass stuck in the air. His muscular cheeks spread wide in an erotic pose. Andrew couldn't take his eyes off those muscular shoulders and back and that perfect line from nape to ass.

Connor worked his way lower until those slick balls rested on his nose, and his tongue worked to that sweet spot. Roughly, Connor grabbed behind both knees and pushed Andrew's legs high into the air.

"That's better," he said as Andrew's ass cheeks opened up, revealing his prize, before he dove in tongue first.

Moans escaped Andrew's lips as he grabbed the covers in his clenched fists. He'd only experienced this once before, but he knew this was the best thing he'd ever felt. It had to be his new favorite, even more than having his dick sucked.

Reaching for his swollen cock, he spread his legs wide so he could get a good grip. He pushed his knees against Connor's strong hands, opening himself up, then gave a stroke or two before Connor dropped one leg.

"Ugh," Andrew moaned as Connor slapped his hand away from his cock.

Sliding up his body, Connor kissed Andrew as the tip of his cock suddenly pushed against his wet hole.

Andrew had no words to describe the sudden sensations that made its way through him. The raw lust of wanting Connor and wanting all of him in him as deep as he could be. Of wanting his hands, mouth, and cock to consume all of him, but then the nerves started to take over.

Connor gently pushed, and his cockhead pressed further into Andrew, bringing a moan of pleasure that he'd never felt. He gave him a needy kiss, then slowly made his way to his neck with soft, teasing kisses as his nose pressed into that spot behind his ear.

"Oh, fuck," Andrew moaned when Connor suddenly pulled off his neck and from between his cheeks.

"Wha—" Andrew's eyes flew open, meeting Connor's. He tried to pull him back down onto him as Connor lifted farther up.

"That will be my birthday present." Connor smiled down at him as he slid his hairy legs over Andrew's smooth ones.

"This is yours." Connor lifted that massive cock and rolled a condom down it before the unmistakable *pop* of a lube lid echoed through the quiet room. Andrew just watched Connor expertly go about his administrations until Connor placed his cockhead against his hole. Sitting up, he stared into Andrew's eyes and face, watching every emotion.

"Um, so fucking big," Connor moaned as the head popped in. He hissed at the sudden pain of his first fuck in a long time. Andrew mirrored that hiss in the pleasure of his first fuck ever.

Connor slowly started to sit.

"Holy fuck!" Andrew moaned as the warmth and tightness enveloped him.

"You're...so...big," Connor grunted as he sank to the base. "Give me a moment to adjust."

Andrew just lay there in complete shock and awe. Pure pleasure held him, and his instinct demanded that his hips start moving.

Connor leaned over and kissed Andrew as he lifted himself up and back down, bringing sounds of ecstasy from Andrew.

After a few moments of riding Andrew's cock, he grabbed him and rolled over onto his back. Pulling his legs up and wide, Andrew sank deep into him.

Andrew's body knew what to do. He started thrusting fast.

"There ya go," Connor sighed blissfully, then reached around for his hips. "Now, long and slow," he instructed.

Andrew complied and pulled his cock out until it was just the tip, then plunged back into Connor with an, "Oh, fuck!"

Connor could see that he was not going to last. Andrew had already been reaching for his cock before Connor sat on his thick dick.

Reaching down, Connor took his dick in hand and started jacking off until Andrew grabbed his hand, pushing him away. Taking Connor's dick, Andrew rubbed the tip with his thumb, smearing the precum around, and used it as lube to jack him off.

"Oh, my God." Connor watched Andrew for a few strokes when he felt his orgasm build. "Fuck yeah, Drew," he moaned. "Fuck me!"

Andrew pulled out and plunged in deep, faster and faster, his hips matching the rhythm of his hand as he stared down into Connor's eyes. His cock started to throb and swell as Connor's ass gripped his dick. His body took over, and he fucked Connor for all he was worth.

Cum exploded from Connor's dick, and he cried out in pleasure. "Fuck me," Connor called out as his hips bucked and his cock spasmed with shot after shot of warm jizz.

Andrew pulled out and plunged deep as he exploded inside Connor. Screaming out in pleasure, he pulled out before plunging in another shot after shot until he fell on Connor's sweaty cum-covered body.

Chest heaving, sweat dripping, and exhausted, they lay there unmoving for a long time before Connor whispered, "Happy birthday, love."

Chapter 8

The following weeks were college midterms, and they were also busy getting everything ready for the Thanksgiving celebration at the Kitchen. Many hours were put into studying, many more hours put into organizing all the foodstuff, the volunteers, and finding time to help Becky with the last bit of her art show.

She had been willing to put together a food collection starring Connor as the nude model with food strategically placed so that he was covered, but he was not going for it at all.

"I don't understand," Andrew said one brisk morning as he and Becky prepped her show's space.

"Yeah, he has a background with the whole picture thing, so he shies away from it if possible."

"But he could do so much good with just a single photograph!" Andrew waved his hands around at her artwork. "One of your paintings and one of his pictures did a world of good. Think about it, all the good both of you could do if you sold a few more pieces of your art!"

"I know." Becky finished dusting the stand with the mosaic sculpture of a medieval head. "One day, maybe, he'll tell you the whole story and why it is such a big deal for him."

"There's a story?" Andrew asked.

"There is always a story!" She laughed and moved on to the next pedestal.

Three days later, midterms were complete, and the art show was on. Andrew took Connor's hand when they entered the space, which was filled with people.

"This is amazing!" Andrew looked around in awe.

"First time to one of these things, huh?" Connor smiled at him.

"You know it is." He smiled, then spied Jack over in the corner, talking to Becky, and waved.

"Hey!" Jack came over and gave them hugs. "So glad to see you! Becky has been a nervous wreck all afternoon!"

"She is always a wreck until the doors open and the space floods with people, and then she is all charm and oozing charisma."

"You know her so well," Jack said cheerfully. "For a few moments, I thought she was going to vomit all over the space that I'd just cleaned. I was going to have to choke her before we opened the doors if she did." He laughed.

Connor shot Andrew a look, mouthing *Wow!* Wide-eyed, they wandered through the gallery. They saw a lot of Connor and Becky's friends, and a few people he knew from working at the Kitchen with them.

In the middle of the entire collection, they stopped before an abstract sculpture four feet tall, with intricate forms that swirled and blended together.

"This is amazing." Andrew looked at it from all sides.

"You like this?"

"Becky! I love it!" Andrew said, hugging her.

"Truly amazing," Connor agreed as he took it in, walking the circumference slowly.

"It looks as though all of these *strands* come from the base and combine to make a type of bleeding heart. If you look at the color here," Andrew pointed. "But then, if you keep moving up, the pieces separate and come back together in a strange kiss."

"Amalgamate," Becky and Connor said at the same time. They looked at each other and smiled.

"When many parts come together to combine but then keep separate to keep their own identity," Becky explained.

"It's amazing," Andrew said.

"I'm glad you think so." She gave a bright smile. "I called it 'Connor.' "

Surprised shock crossed his face. "What?"

"Well, there is so much of a story here, and it was a long journey. You've been my inspiration for this masterpiece."

"I'm flattered, but I'm certainly not a masterpiece," Connor said, rolling his eyes.

"That's not how I felt. I feel that it is a true masterpiece." A deep voice rolled over them from behind.

Everyone turned to the stranger. Mirrored shock crossed both Becky and Connor's faces when they saw the imposing, tall, dark, and handsome man. Andrew thought it was such a cliché thing to say, but he was taller than Connor. He had black hair, tanned skin, a perfect smile, and the whitest teeth Andrew had ever seen.

"When I bought it, I knew that the sculpture was everything that the artist intended for it to be. A description of a love so deep that the ability to keep an inkling of oneself was, well, impossible."

Andrew heard movement and turned to see Connor gone. He gave Becky a questioning look and then left to find Connor.

"Hey, you okay?" Andrew asked when he saw Connor standing outside the doorway in the cold night air without his coat. He was hunched over, and his breathing had turned erratic.

"Yeah, sorry. I just, umm, I suddenly felt nauseous. Thought I might be sick, so I came out here to get some fresh air to help."

"You should have told me you weren't feeling the greatest." Andrew rubbed his back lovingly. "I'd never have made that Spicy Chicken Curry."

A weak smile, Connor took his hand and squeezed. "It definitely wasn't the curry chicken. That was the most amazing dish ever!"

"But your stomach."

"Just nervous, I think." Connor stood and then stretched his shoulders and waist.

"Nervous?"

"Yeah, nervous." Connor looked down. "Tomorrow, you're leaving for the holidays. Going back to your parents."

Connor reached out, took Andrew's hands, squeezed them, and pulled him into a tight embrace. Resting his head atop Andrew's, he could feel the shivers of cold course through him.

"You look amazing tonight," Connor murmured.

"Thank you." Connor could feel Andrew smile into his chest.

"I'm going to miss you." Connor hugged him tighter. "The company, the laughs, the food—"

"There it is," Andrew laughed, looking up at Connor.

"I'll miss this," Connor said, leaning down to gently kiss Andrew. His arms tightened, crushing their bodies together.

Andrew didn't know how long they stood there kissing, but when it came to an end, he groaned.

"It'll only be until Saturday," Andrew said.

"I know."

"And you'll have the Kitchen over Thanksgiving to keep you busy," Andrew smiled. "And you'll have Becky to annoy the goodness out of you and Alma to keep you almost in line."

Connor laughed.

"I can see your breath. You look like an ice dragon huffing and puffing." Andrew gave him a teasing smile.

"Ice dragon? Do they devour the damsel in distress?"

"Did you call me a damsel?" Andrew feigned outrage.

"Well, you see—"

"I'll show you my damsel." Andrew pressed his groin into Connor's leg.

"Oh, my." Connor looked around. "I think me that we need to go take care of that!"

"Here?" Andrew's voice broke in surprise.

Connor laughed, taking him by the hand and walking down the street to their home.

Entering the house, they made it to the couch; their shirts and shoes had already been haphazardly discarded across the living space. The sounds of kissing and needed grunts of lust echoed through the house as they groped and clawed at each other.

Never missing a kiss, Andrew unbuttoned his pants and had them off quickly, laying down naked on Connor, who grabbed an ass cheek in one hand and hard cock in the other.

"Holy fuck, your hands are cold!" Andrew tried to wriggle from his grasp.

"Ice Dragon," Connor hissed out, holding on tight. "So warm me up." He kissed those full lips, administering another round of jacking and groping.

Andrew kissed down his chest to his nipples and started to suck and nibble as he unbuttoned Connor's pants. Sitting back, he pulled the pants and briefs down, but before he pulled them off, he pushed Connor's legs up and pulled his cock down between his legs.

"What?" Connor tried to move his legs, but his pants and briefs were tight around his ankles. Andrew's mouth wrapped around his cock.

"Oh fuck, that feels amazing," Connor murmured, trying to reach up and get rid of his pants, but when he got close, Andrew pushed his legs farther up as his face sank into his ass.

Flicking his tongue around Connor's hole, he rimmed him fast and wet, producing sounds of lust from Connor.

Connor felt Andrew pull out of his ass and heard him spit before his tongue found its place in his hole. After rimming his hole until it was wet and ready, Andrew climbed to his knees and lined up his cock.

"Wait," Connor panted. He wanted to feel Andrew in him, and he wanted it now, but instead, he said, "We need a condom and lube."

Andrew paused with lusty indecision. "You're the only one I've ever been with."

"I know. Let's be smart and get tested. We've nothing to fear, but just in case."

Andrew's drive started to wilt. His firm cock started to sag.

"Hey." Connor's strong hands caressed Andrew's neck and face. "Nothing to fear, but if there is that slight chance? I could never live with myself if something ever happened to you, and I was the cause."

"Ok," Andrew nodded and quickly disappeared into the darkness of their bedroom. The ripping of the condom package and the popping of the lube bottle were almost simultaneously done, and when Andrew took hold of Connor's feet and placed his cock at his entrance, he was ready.

Sliding his dick head around that wet hole, Andrew started to push in and then pulled out, enjoying Connor's moans of disappointment before pressing in again. When Connor started to open up, he pulled out again.

"Tease!" Connor groaned. "Give it to me!"

"Now I've got you right where I want you." Andrew grinned, pulling the pants from around Connor's ankles. Before Connor could open his legs, Andrew took his foot and put it to his mouth to lick his toes while never breaking eye contact.

Inserting one toe in his mouth, he started to suck on it as he pushed into Connor. The moan that escaped his beautiful lips said it all. Moving to the next toe, he sank to the base and held still there while moving to the next toe, listening to Connor's moans.

Pushing his legs wide, Andrew started fucking in long, strong strokes from tip to taint. His large balls slapped against Connor's ass.

"That's amazing," Connor moaned, and Andrew started fucking faster. Staring deep into his man's eyes, Andrew ran his dainty hands down Connor's thighs, opening him up further. Taking hold of his hips, Andrew fucked, hard, and Connor called out in rapture.

Andrew leaned down to crush their lips together, and Connor shot jizz between them. The shocked moan came from Connor as he wrapped his strong arms around Andrew and bucked his hips as another shot of cum flooded between them.

Pulling almost all the way out, Andrew plunged in with a hard thrust and shot his load into the tight ass that gripped his cock.

Connor's grip on him loosened, and Andrew fell onto his chest, exhausted. His hard cock was still in Connor; they lay together, breathing each other in.

"That was amazing," Andrew whispered into Connor's chest.

"I've never done that."

"What?"

"Orgasmed hands free. That was seriously amazing. I was so excited and so into you and your aggressiveness that I just came."

"It was hot. Feeling you come on my dick did it for me."

They lay together, enjoying the moment and reveling in each other. Andrew exhausted against Connor, who lightly caressed Andrew's back and arms with his fingertips.

"I've never had my toes sucked, but we'll need to explore this a little more. That was so hot."

"Yeah? You liked it?"

"Definitely."

"I've been wanting to try that. For some reason, the thought of you on your back, my cock in you while sucking on your toes . . ." Andrew's cock twitched as if coming back to life.

"Whoa, mister." Conner squeezed his hips and his ass gripped Andrew. "Think you're up for round two?"

"Umm, maybe." Andrew chuckled, pulling his hips backward until he fell out. "I'll run us a shower."

"Oh? That's promising." Connor smiled, leaning in for a kiss as Andrew got to his feet.

Afterward, showered clean and dried off, Connor lay in bed with Andrew draped over him. Rubbing his back with just his fingertips, absentmindedly tickling him as they drifted off to sleep, Andrew thought he heard, "I love you," before sleep took him.

Chapter 9

Andrew had been on the road for two hours and still had two to go. He adjusted the radio, but nothing would come through except old, twangy country and bible music. With a deep breath, he connected his phone and settled in with some modern music. The weather was unusually cold for this time of the year, and the forecast was for Thanksgiving snow.

It's too early for that. Ugh, I hate the cold! He thought when he saw the rest stop sign. Pulling over, he decided to grab a soda and a pee and stretch his legs for a moment before the next two hours in the car.

Running from the car to the rest stop, he went to the urinal and started to pee when he realized the guy two urinals down was looking in his direction. Nervous sweat started to bead on his forehead, but his cock began to chub up.

Stop it! told himself. The guy was probably just looking around while he peed, but he'd been there when he walked into the restroom. Then he realized that he'd seen only one car in the parking lot, and there hadn't been anyone in the lobby.

Taking a deep breath, he stared down at his cock and pushed, trying to pee faster. The more he watched his cock, the fatter it was getting, so he exhaled and looked to the ceiling, trying to ignore the guy.

Why are you doing this? He chastised his penis. *We just had a whole night of Connor, and you don't need a stranger's attention in a local rest stop, for Christ's sake.*

Besides, he'd always thought he was straight and that he'd make a life with Cassie before he'd met Connor. *Besides that one night with Jeremy…* His cock twitched at the thought of them on the riverbank in the darkness.

His penis raised up to stick straight out.

"How's it going?" The stranger's deep voice resonated in the quiet bathroom.

"Um, fine." Andrew tried to look anywhere except the stranger.

"Long drive?"

"Not terribly, no."

"Need some relief to help you get through?"

Andrew looked at the guy, shocked he was so brazenly open. Then he quickly glanced down, and the guy was gently stroking his rock-hard cock.

"No, no, thank you," Andrew said, turning from him.

"Are you sure?"

"Yes," Andrew whispered.

"I think your cock has a different opinion." The stranger smiled, then licked his lips suggestively. "Mmm, and a big one too," he almost purred.

Finished peeing, he tried to put his hard cock away, which was challenging, but he managed it.

"We can make it quick, or I can take my time, and I swallow."

"I've got a boyfriend, and you look like my dad." Andrew didn't look at him. "That weirds me out."

"Boyfriend's not here, and I can definitely get into some daddy-son roleplay." The man smirked. "Daddy's been caught, and son needs to show him a lesson by taking it out on his ass."

Andrew tried not to vomit in his mouth as he left the bathroom as quickly as he could, grabbed a soda before the guy could come out and suggest anything else, lewd or public, ran to his car.

As he drove away, he realized that he'd called Connor his boyfriend, and that brought a smile to his face. It was the first time that he'd used the term.

Ever.

The word, boyfriend, made him feel good. The feelings that it invoked in him brought a smile to his face. He thought of Connor longingly. His hugs, his kisses, his strong arms wrapped around him. The way he gave a slight moan when he pulled a fork from his mouth, tasting a dessert he'd specially made him.

The way his chest rose and fell when he took a deep, relaxing breath while he slept as Andrew lay there, listening to the beat of his heart.

"I'm in love." Andrew realized as he drove down the lonely highway.

He'd been too close to the situation when he'd been at college, but now that he was away, he couldn't stop thinking about Connor. Couldn't stop thinking about every move, breath, and noise he made. The way he smelled of fresh pine on a wintry morning. *How does that even happen?*

He didn't know, but it excited him.

The rest of the drive, he thought about his boyfriend, Connor, with a bright smile. Then he turned into the driveway to his parents' home. A little nervous, he prayed this was going to go okay.

The first three days had gone well, but they had been busy. Dad had still worked until Wednesday, and Mom was busy getting ready to prepare the meal for Thanksgiving. They'd invited Grampa, who was coming over on the day before to, as he put it, get in the way, and then there were siblings and cousins galore. Andrew's parents had been the only ones to have one child. The rest had rabbit syndrome.

Andrew spent a few days with some of his friends he hadn't seen since he moved to university. A few had already heard of his and Cassie's breakup, and apparently, Cassie had already told her side of the story to some as well. Of course, the story always had two sides, and his side had been left out.

Mikey, Jim, and Joe had all been good with him when he explained what had happened. He didn't tell them any details except that they'd broken up and he had a new roommate in Connor. After they'd been fed Cassie's drama, Justin and John wouldn't have anything to do with him.

Then there was Derek. He had been one of Andrew's best friends for as long as he could remember. He had also been good friends with Cassie, and he'd told Andrew about how Cassie had come home from college right after Halloween. She'd been released from school—their choice, not hers—over an incident at a party.

Andrew watched his friend closely. He knew Derek had strong opinions on male and female relations and was not afraid to voice those opinions. He was not one to back down, and he could be belligerent in his right to tell his version of the truth.

There's one in every group.

Derek gave Andrew one chance. He hadn't been subtle or coy in looking Andrew up and down, asking, "So, is it true? You a fag?"

"I don't think I can say," Andrew said warily. "I have been with—"

"You sleep with men?"

There it was. Andrew could feel the sweat bead up on his forehead, his heart racing in his chest, and the blood pounding through his neck and behind his ears. He felt like he was about to pass out.

"Everyone already knows," Derek said. "Cass came home and told us all what happened. You left her for a guy and then helped get her kicked out of college."

"I did leave her, but not for a guy. I left for my dignity and sanity. She was kicked out of college on her own, and I won't be blamed for that." Andrew decided he would not back down.

He'd always been the timid one. He'd always been the one to go along with the plan, and if someone took something out on him, he took it. He'd been that way with his friends, he'd been that way with Cassie, and he'd been that way with his family.

No more! Enough is enough, and I deserve better!

"So, are you fucking a dude?"

He was fixated on the question. There was no talking to him, Andrew realized. He would keep circling back to the same question no matter what else was thrown out there. He wanted his truths so he could place Andrew into a box labeled 'homo' and be able to move on with his hate.

"I hope you find peace in your hate." Andrew met his cold stare for a moment, then turned and walked away.

Now, he was back at his parents' house and helping his mother in the kitchen while she prepared what she could for Thursday. He loved to listen to her hum and quietly sing as she baked her pies. The smell of the heat from the oven when she would open and close it to adjust her pies, the way she'd almost glide to get her ingredients, and the tiny smear of flour that always ended up on her cheek.

A sadness came over him that was just as strong as the happiness when he pulled into the driveway.

They would find out sooner rather than later, and it wasn't his choice to tell them. Cassie had taken that from him. But why did it have to be said? Straight people didn't go around announcing they were straight, and he would not conform to having to announce something about himself.

He didn't one day walk up to everyone and say, "Everyone, I have brown eyes." So he definitely wasn't going to walk up to people and tell them he slept with men.

"Son."

Andrew felt his heart stop.

"Son!"

Andrew felt like he was having an out-of-body experience. He was floating there watching the body, his body, slowly turning and looking in the direction of the dining room. He slowly stood and turned even though his instinct told him not to.

"Yeah, Dad?" His voice sounded foreign and forced. *He knows*, Andrew's mind screamed. He tried to shake the feeling off, but the way Dad had called him into the room. *Somethings wrong!*

"Can you come in here a moment?"

Andrew walked into the room, and his grandpa and dad were sitting at the table. They looked like stone statues staring at him.

"Sit."

His dad had never been one for many words, but this was unlike him. Andrew pulled out a chair and slowly sat.

"What's going on, dear? Dad?" his mom asked, confused.

"We're going to have a man-to-man with Andrew, honey. It won't take long." His dad forced a smile for his wife. "Nothing to concern yourself with."

She nodded and went back to the kitchen and her pies.

"Is it true?"

"Dale." Grampa glanced at his son-in-law, and Andrew could see the warning in those gray eyes.

"Is it true you're gay?" His dad was right to the point in his disbelieving anger.

"Dale," Grampa said, leaning back in his chair with a slight shake of his head. "I didn't ask you to come get me a day early so we could be the Spanish Inquisition, dammit. I wanted to be here in case it snowed, and I couldn't get out."

"Marvin—" Dale side-eyed his father-in-law.

"Does it matter, son?" his grampa asked without taking his eyes off his son-in-law, drumming his thumb rapidly on the table as he did so often. The sound brought a smile to Andrew's face.

He did the same thing while cooking and trying to figure out the ingredients. It was the first time Andrew realized that, and it made him happy to realize how much alike he was to his grampa.

"Yeah, it does," Dad suddenly said.

"No, it doesn't."

"It does to me, dammit."

"Why? So you can preach to the boy?" Grampa rolled his eyes. "Let him be."

"Seriously?"

"You did things to disappoint your daddy, son. I remember the day you told him you were not joining the military. You didn't want to, and he wouldn't make you. You'd met a young lady that had turned your head, and you were making good money at the factory."

"That isn't the same thing." Dad clenched his fist.

"Why isn't it?" Grampa leaned back in his chair, took a long sip of his steaming hot coffee, and gave Andrew a sligh wink. "Disappointment is disappointment. No matter what it is over or how you look at it. The emotion is the same."

"No."

"I know you're not going to cause a fuss about this, Dale. Look at the boy, our boy. If he is loved and he loves someone back in a respectable relationship, that is all we can ask in this world."

"Changed your tune, Dad?"

"I've learned some things over the years. Patience, kindness, loneliness, joy, and how not to give a shit when it doesn't involve me."

There was a long pause before Grampa said, "All these people running around posting on their phones about Lord-knows-what and screaming about all the injustices of the world. Then tomorrow, something else offends them. They don't remember what they were preaching yesterday because they are preaching something different today. Chasing their tails round and round in a never-ending cycle."

"Dad?" Andrew suddenly surprised himself by speaking. He'd been enjoying listening to his grampa tell his dad. Grampa seemed to be the only one in the world who could tell his dad anything.

Andrew made direct eye contact and held his father's gaze.

"I don't know what you are looking for because it isn't simple. Am I gay? Am I straight? Does it matter? I was with Cassie—" He paused for a moment, pulling his strength to center himself. "Now I'm with Connor."

"There, I told you." Dale slapped his hand down on the table.

"Told me what? That Cassie was a crazy who treated your boy like shit?" Grampa set his coffee on the table and leveled his gaze. "Isn't that what you kept telling me? How you wished our boy would grow some man balls to see what kind of person she really was? How you knew he loved her but didn't know what he saw in her and didn't want to drive him away by speaking the truth? Well, hopefully, this Connor is a fine young man who treats our boy with decency and respect, and that isn't anything less than he deserves!"

Dad gaped at Grampa.

"Isn't that what you told me, son?" Grampa licked his lips and then took a drink of his coffee. "You telling me you'd rather him stay with a crazy like Cassie? Just the other day, I saw her down at the fillin' station. Lord, help that one." Grampa gave a sad, disappointed shake of his head for whatever he'd witnessed.

"Dad," Dale said.

"He is young, yeah?" Grampa looked at me. "He's a young man?"

"You know any women who go by Connor?" Dale exasperated.

"I just don't want some, what do they call them, son?" Grampa looked at me. "Some man-cougar, hunting you down."

Andrew laughed.

He laughed so hard that tears streamed from his eyes as his dad and grampa stared at him like he'd gone and lost his mind.

"Grampa, I love you," he said between peals of laughter.

It took a long moment, but he was able to get himself under control finally. The giggles flared up again, but he was able to control them. Wiping the tears from his face and meeting his dad's eyes, he said, "I'll go back to college to give you some space."

"Son, I've got your dad in hand. He won't be giving you any trouble."

"Thank you, Grampa, but I don't want him to be uncomfortable in his own home. I'll tell Mom something. I forgot to feed the cat." Andrew waved his hand nonchalantly. "I'll make something up."

Andrew got up and gave his grandpa the biggest hug. "Thank you," he whispered. Then he went to make his excuses to his mom, all the while hearing his grandpa berate his dad.

At the door, Andrew turned. "Dad, I still love you. You're my dad, and you always will be. One day, I hope you can be as proud to be my dad as I am to be your son."

With that, he left. His dad did not stop him.

***

He'd been on the road for two hours and needed to pee when he passed the sign for the rest stop in ten miles.

"Lord, let it be empty," Andrew murmured.

There were a few cars in the lot. People who were traveling before the holiday. They were standing in the cold, stretching it out, or letting their kids and dogs run for a moment to release some of the energy so they didn't drive Mom and Dad crazy.

Walking into the lobby, Andrew looked around and mall-walked to the men's restroom on the other side of the building. He made it to the urinal and hauled out his penis. A strong stream erupted with a much-needed sigh.

"Knew you'd come back, son," a voice said as a man saddled up next to him at the urinal.

"Fuck," Andrew muttered.

"We can do that too." The man's slimy voice oozed from him as he stroked the length of his cock. "Mmm, daddy's boy has a big peepee—"

"Don't touch my penis!" Andrew yelled at the top of his lungs. The man jerked back from him, trying to put his cock away as the attendant ran into the restroom.

"You!!" He grabbed hold of the man, who was holding his semi-hard dick. "I've been trying to catch you," the attendant said as he tried hauling the man from the bathroom. The stranger jerked around as he put his dick back into his pants and tried escaping the restroom with the attendant grabbing his arm.

Andrew smiled and finished pissing in peace—except for the echoing yells of the man being hauled from the building.

For the next two hours, Andrew chuckled to himself, first thinking about his grampa and how he'd stood up for Andrew and Connor. Second, he laughed at the lewd man and the crazy experience he'd never in a million years dream he'd have. He couldn't wait to tell Connor everything that had happened.

He drove up to the Kitchen parking lot, got out into the cold, wrapped his coat around him, and ran in as fast as possible. As he entered, the little bell going off made him smile with giddiness of seeing his boyfriend. That thought alone, such a foreign thing so many months ago that he would've denied, now brought him endless joy.

"Just me," he called out as he entered the kitchen, where everyone was prepping food for their Thanksgiving dinner.

"Hey." Andrew smiled, giving Alma the biggest hug and then making his way to Jack. "I couldn't let you all go through Thanksgiving without me." He smiled at them, bright and cheerful.

"Went bad, didn't it?" Jack had a disappointed frown as he rubbed Andrew's upper arms.

"Cassie went back and told everyone her version, and it was a tough few days," Andrew confided.

"If you need to vent, I'll understand more than most." Jack gave him a sad smile.

"But you said that—"

"Bullshit," Jack admitted. "It was all bullshit so that you wouldn't know the truth. The only family I've got is right here in this kitchen."

Andrew gave him a fierce hug. "And we are the only family you need."

"Oh." Becky's look of surprise when she came around the corner and saw Andrew was almost glaringly in your face.

"Hey, Bek!" Andrew grabbed the box from her hand. "Let me help you with this."

"Thanks."

"Yeah, no prob." Andrew smiled. "Hey, where's Connor? I have to tell him about my grampa. It was the damnedest thing! And this guy in the bathroom that got arrested . . ."

"He ran home to shower," Becky said, pulling out her phone. "I'll call him real quick and let him know you're here."

"It's fine," Andrew said, turning for the door. "I'll surprise him—in the shower," Andrew sang with a little shimmy of the shoulders accompanied by a suggestive wiggle of his brows and he was gone before anyone could say another word.

He drove to the apartment in anticipation of seeing Connor, his boyfriend. The smile on his face almost hurt. His heart beat faster with excitement at the idea of getting into the shower with him. Thinking of the steamy, wet air and Connor's hot body made him hard.

Taking the stairs two at a time, Andrew entered the apartment, pulling off his coat and throwing it onto the island. He could hear the shower going and started to untuck his shirt as he walked into the bedroom and stopped.

Connor walked in from the bathroom with a towel around his naked, wet body. The total look of surprise on his face when Andrew walked in was evident.

Then Andrew noticed the man on the bed. A naked man with a raging hard cock sticking straight up. His breath caught in his chest, and tears flooded his eyes. There, nude, in their bed was mister tall, dark, and handsome from the gallery.

Chapter 10

Andrew sat in his car, staring at the snow that started to fall as tears fell from his eyes. He'd been at the park for an hour and couldn't do anything but cry.

It hurt.

It hurt worse than when he'd walked up on Cassie being fucked on the riverbank.

At one point, he couldn't breathe and got out of the car, knowing he was close to passing out from asphyxiation. He leaned back on the car, trying to pull the cold air into his lungs and exhaling slowly, but his anxiety would not let him, and he fell to his knees, sobbing with his face in his hands.

At long last, he managed to pull himself together. Part of it had to do with the cold, wet snow invading his warmth. Seeping through his jeans, making his knees and legs go numb. After he climbed to his feet and gulped several deep breaths, he got back into his car and drove off. He'd been on the road for two hours and had stopped at the rest stop. He didn't know what to do. He'd pulled over because it was dark, and he couldn't see from the tears that just wouldn't stop.

A numbness grew inside his chest as the world seemed to fade. It was just him, the cold, and the darkness as he stared into the void before him.

A tap on his window startled him awake. His eyes barely opened. He could feel that they were red and swollen. More than that, every muscle ached from the position he'd fallen asleep in the driver's seat.

"Son, you okay?" The officer outside his car tapped on the window again.

A groan escaped Andrew, and he tried to pull the seat up. The car was still running. He must've let it run all night. He was almost out of gas.

Andrew opened the door and slowly climbed from the car, his every muscle echoing his groan as he moved them.

"Son, you all right?" the officer said as he inspected Andrew's face. "The attendant called and let us know you'd been here all night. He said that you'd stopped here yesterday morning, and then when he showed up this morning, you were back."

"Yes, officer." Andrew wrapped his arms around him when the freezing air hit him.

"Old Joe said something about an incident with a guy in the restroom?"

"Yes, officer," Andrew murmured.

"Well, if you wouldn't mind, I could take down your information, and if we could call you so you could pick him out of a lineup, we'd appreciate it. We've been trying to catch him for a while. He keeps propositioning people in the bathroom. I'm surprised one of these truckers hasn't beat the shit out of him." The officer chuckled.

"Hey." Now, the officer looked concerned. "You sure you're okay?"

"Just a rough day yesterday, and I'd been driving too long. I thought it was safer to pull over and get some sleep instead of trying to push through," Andrew explained.

"Smart move. I always tell my son the same thing. I don't care what happens; if you're tired, you pull over and rest before trying to force it. I've seen too many accidents on this highway to count, and I always hear how tired they were, but they were too close to home to stop."

Andrew followed the officer inside and gave him his information. He went to the restroom and splashed cold water on his face. He almost didn't recognize himself when he looked into the mirror.

Red, swollen eyes, his complexion paler than normal, and a heartbroken look about him. He didn't know where he was going to go. He couldn't go back to college. He didn't want to be around anyone but didn't know where to go.

After yesterday, he couldn't go to his parents' house, but he could go to his grandpa's.

"The cabin," he whispered. His grandpa had a cabin that wasn't too far a drive from where he was. They used to go there every summer for years, and it was vacant now. He could stay there until he figured out how he was going to move forward.

Andrew ran back to his car through the freezing winter air. It was not the first time he'd cursed himself for leaving his coat on the island when he'd run out of the apartment.

Driving down the road, Andrew stopped at a local grocery store and picked up a few items he was sure he would need. The cabin was always stocked with some necessities, but his grampa didn't usually go up there in the winter. It took him another two hours to get to the driveway off the state highway.

The driveway, if you could call it that, was rough and not well-maintained. It was more of a treelined logging trail that would admit only one car at a time and only had one spot where two cars could get around each other. Andrew pulled up to the cabin after three miles of bumpy, slow-going careful driving.

It wasn't very big, but it was cozy with all had of this place—of the laughs and the hot summers spent here, of hiking through the forest, fishing in the river, and even ice skating on the pond.

This was where his grampa escaped from life, and this was where he would do the same until he could figure out his place in the world.

After finding the key under the rock, Andrew climbed the stairs to the porch and went inside. The cabin only had three rooms. A bedroom, a bathroom, and a cozy living space big enough for a kitchen, table, and a sofa before the fireplace.

Discarding his groceries, he went to work opening the flue before lighting a fire in the fireplace. With a little heat emanating off the fresh fire Andrew lit the furnace so he could have some heat and hot water. Going through, he took the sheets off the furniture so he could be comfortable and then decided to take a long hot shower once the water was heated.

He stood with the water cascading over him. Feeling the steam rising all around him as the hot water poured down, he cried.

He had never been one to cry, but then again, he'd never had his heart broken like this before. He tried not to even think about Connor or the naked man on their bed, but the images just kept coming back to him.

So, he decided to spend the shower time crying. He would get all of it out of his system, and then build himself back up.

Once the water started to turn cold, he shut it off and shut down the tears. He dried off and went out into the cabin. He would have to dress in his dirty clothes unless his grampa had left something behind, but then he remembered he was alone. He was the only one here.

"Nude it is," he said to himself.

Once his meager dinner of chips and a sandwich were done, the light of day faded past dusk into night. He had his meal, found a bottle of whiskey, and took out one of his gramma's puzzles. She had loved doing puzzles and would sit for hours muttering to herself before she'd get up and move about, making dinner or whatever. But she would always walk back to the puzzle and look at it from a different angle to find a missing piece.

Half a bottle of whiskey later, having worked on the puzzle until late, he settled into the couch and let the warmth of the fire soothe him to sleep.

Waking up groggy, Andrew looked around, at first not remembering where he was. Then, the memories of the last two days came rushing back. Pulling himself together before he could loose control of his emotions, Andrew told himself that was the old him and the new him was here to stay.

It was Wednesday, and tomorrow was Thanksgiving. He would not slink back home with his tail between his legs so his dad could pull an 'I told you so' moment. He would spend the next few days here, alone. Then, he would travel back to school and figure out his living situation.

He would talk to Jack first, but he knew it would only be temporary. Andrew knew Jack had a crush on him and didn't need that in his life right now. He needed to focus on the rest of this semester and the next. Then he would have one year to go until graduation with his bachelor's degree.

"Where will I go?" he asked himself.

This was a whole new concept. He'd always known he'd finish college, marry Cassie, and move back to his hometown to raise their American Dream.

That dream was dead and buried.

He could go anywhere, and he could do anything. He was twenty-two and had never seen the ocean. He could travel to Florida and find a job on the beach. Live day to day in the sand and on the water while making desserts.

Andrew spent the morning hiking through the woods and just being by himself. He'd always enjoyed his own company, and this time was good for him. Once the temperature fell and the snow started falling again, he made his way back to the cabin, took a hot shower, had dinner, and finished his puzzle before throwing a few more logs on the fire and settling down for the night.

Waking up on Thanksgiving, Andrew realized he hadn't looked at his phone once since he'd run out of the apartment. Honestly, he didn't even know where his phone was, but he would have to call his mom and wish her a Happy Thanksgiving, or she would worry to death.

He found his phone in the car, between his console and his seat; it was dead. He plugged it into the car charger and went about his day the same way he had yesterday, alone with his thoughts and the freedom to just be.

After another day of hiking in the woods, he showered, made dinner, and took up another glass of whiskey. Settling into the sofa with a blanket over his legs and a cold drink in his hands, he watched the flames dance across the new logs he'd thrown in. The bright orange flames swiveled and swirled, lulling him with its heat into an easy, relaxed sleep.

Firelight flickered through the living room, and the large white snowflakes fell outside the dark window. Just as he was dozing off, the front door slammed open.

In walked Connor.

Chapter 11

"What. The. Fuck!" Connor's voice dominated the entire space. The hood over his head cast shadows on his face, but Andrew could see the bright red tip of his nose and the puffs of breath in the cold air that stole in through the dark doorway.

The door slammed shut, and Connor took two menacing steps into the room. His body was rigid with frozen anger, and his eyes were cold as ice.

"Do you know how worried I've been?" Connor yelled. "Do you know how long I've been looking for you—how many times I've called you!?"

Andrew winced.

Connor's rage was in every crevice of the room. His very presence radiated the anger he felt, and the world around him seemed to bend to his will.

Andrew stood, wrapping the blanket around him tightly like a shield. He didn't want to have this confrontation. He hated confrontation altogether, and he'd planned on working around this until he could graduate and move away.

Connor took three giant steps, wrapping Andrew up in his strong arms.

"I've been so worried." Connor's voice shook, as did his shoulders, and his strong arms squeezed the breath from Andrew.

Connor embraced him for a long moment, then stepped back, holding Andrew at arm's length and looking him up and down.

“Are you hurt?”

“Just my heart,” Andrew found the courage to say. He didn’t want this, but if it was going to be thrust upon him, he would stand up for himself once and for all.

“Drew.” Connor took his face in his hands and crushed their lips together, but Andrew twisted away from him.

Turning his back on Connor, he took a few steps toward the fireplace. The heat was becoming a little much, but he’d endure.

“Just go.” Andrew tried to keep the tears at bay, but they seemed to build up of their own accord.

“I’m not going anywhere,” Connor said. “I’m not going without you. Do you know what I’ve done to find you?”

“What?” Andrew suddenly realized he’d never told Connor about this place.

“I’ve called everyone!” Connor yelled. Andrew didn’t think he realized he was yelling, but his anger was intense.

“Do you know how hard it was for me to call Cassie and ask her if she’d seen you?”

“Why would you do that?” Andrew demanded angrily.

“Because she was listed as your emergency contact at school!”

“How do you know that?”

“I know people, and so does Becky, but it was thanks to Jack and Joannie,” Connor told him. “Jack works in the Administration office and was able to look up your contact. When she refused to tell me, I drove to your parents’ house.”

"You didn't." Andrew had a sinking feeling in the pit of his stomach and went to grab his phone, only to realize it was still in the car on the charger.

"Your dad is furious, and your mom is worried sick."

"Why the fuck would you do that?" Andrew shouted.

Connor took a step back from Andrew. It was the first time he'd ever raised his voice or shown any anger.

"Because I was worried." The steam seemed to deflate from Connor. Tears swelled in his eyes and ran down his red cheeks. "I was so worried, and I couldn't find you. I was worried something bad had happened to you."

"Something bad did happen." Andrew's anger was rising. "You broke my heart!" he screamed.

"Oh, baby—"

"No!" Andrew stepped away from him. "You don't get to fuck the first guy you come across when I'm not there and then try to 'oh baby' me!"

Tears streamed down his face.

"I loved you!" Andrew cried. Sobs racked his body, and he fell to his knees, covering his face so Connor couldn't see how hurt he truly was.

His sobs were so violent he couldn't catch his breath. Andrew knew that he was going to pass out from lack of oxygen, and the pain within his heart radiated throughout his entire body and soul.

Connor's arms were around him, and he was saying something, but Andrew could not comprehend what he said. He sobbed harder because he wanted to fall into those strong arms. He wanted them wrapped around him to protect him from all the hurt the world had to offer, but they were the reason he hurt.

He cried harder.

When all the tears and sobs left him, Andrew felt exhausted. He wanted to curl up in a ball and disappear, but Connor was still draped around him. Holding him.

"Leave," he croaked.

"No."

"Get. Out."

"No."

"Why won't you just go?" Andrew quietly asked.

"Because I love you too," Connor said as if it were the simplest thing in the world. As if it were glaringly obvious. As if it righted the wrong that hurt him.

"Yeah?" Andrew sat up and looked at Connor. "What about mister tall, dark, and raging hard-on in our bed?"

"That was Mitch," Connor slowly stated.

"Oh, well, that makes everything better, doesn't it?" Andrew's sarcasm was pointed.

"Can you just listen for a moment, please?"

Andrew climbed to his feet, wiping his face on his sleeve, and picked up his glass. Downing the whiskey in one shot, he poured himself another and sat on the sofa.

"Do I have a choice?"

"No."

Connor stood watching Andrew, and when he sat, Connor pulled the coffee table back and sat down with his hands on Andrew's knees. He squeezed them and looked Andrew in the eye.

"I didn't cheat on you," he stated flatly.

Andrew's eyebrows shot up.

"I know." Connor took a deep breath and exhaled. "I know what it looked like, but I can tell you that I did not sleep with him, Andrew. I swear it on Aiyden's life."

That got Andrew's attention. He knew nothing about Connor's family life because it was never mentioned, so he never brought it up. He didn't want to bring up anything that would hurt Connor, but he knew that Aiyden was truly special to him.

"Listen…" A sad look crossed Connor's face. He tried to hide it but couldn't keep the pain from showing. "I was new at college when I met Mitch. We started dating, and things were getting serious when my parents got in an accident."

He took a deep breath. "They both died," he stated matter-of-factly.

He swallowed, hard, as if to swallow the pain.

Taking a moment for it to sink in, he started up again. "They were all I had—no grandparents, aunts, or uncles. I was alone in the world and had nothing. No money, no job, no family. I was all alone."

He blinked, then wiped away the tears forming at the corners of his eyes.

"Mitch was all I had, and we had nothing but each other. I studied sports medicine and physical exercise while he studied photography. He took some pictures of me and sold them. I didn't know he'd done it until he bought some items I knew we couldn't afford."

"He never told me that he was selling my photos or, well, his photos of me. When I brought up the crazy purchases, he explained that he had sold some nature photos. He told me he'd entered a contest and won. They liked the photo so much they wanted to see his portfolio and bought several pictures."

Connor took a deep breath.

"I believed him. I believed every word of it," Connor said in a far-off tone. It was as if he were reliving that time in his life, and Andrew could hear the pain in his voice.

"I'm not going to lie, but I definitely enjoyed the attention he lavished upon me. We bought some new cars and clothes, and we bought a house. We were planning on making it ours . . . until one evening," Connor took a hard breath. "I went away to a school function, and when I came home, he was in bed with others."

"Others?" Andrew asked.

"Three other men," Connor nodded. "I was hurt, confused, angry, and every other emotion that Becky could define. She helped me. We were able to get some money from the pictures that he took of me, but he'd tricked me into signing a release waiver without my knowing; he made a lot of money off me."

"That's why you didn't want Becky to take your picture?" Andrew asked, putting the pieces together.

"Right," Connor confirmed. "So, I bought his portion of the house and was going to sell it when we stumbled upon Aiyden. So then I thought, what better way to give back to the world and set up a legacy for others?

"I didn't have anything, and I didn't necessarily want the money because it reminded me of what had been done to me. So, I put it to good use."

"That's commendable." Andrew wiped his nose on his sleeve.

"Thanks." Connor's sad smile said it all. "Mitch came back and wanted to make up. He apologized and tried to get me back. I told him to go to hell and went to play some sand volleyball to get my mind off him."

"That's when I met you." Connor squeezed his legs.

"But why was he in our bed?" Andrew asked skeptically. For a moment, he'd been drawn into the story and had forgotten the reason for their being at his grampa's cabin in the first place. He'd caught another man in their bed.

Connor laughed and looked to the ceiling. "He bought Becky's sculpture. We saw him that night, and that's why I left. I confronted Becky and told her what I thought about her selling that to him, but she hadn't known it was him. He bought it through another name. Some company of his, or so we gathered. She made a lot of money off him and that piece."

"He came to me after you'd left, and I told him to get lost. Then he came to me, again and again, and I told him to fuck off. I was at the Kitchen, and Alma tripped, spilling hot soup all over me. I'd taken my clothes off and went home to shower."

"Honestly," Connor emphasized his words by squeezing his legs. "I was in the shower and heard something. I came out of the bathroom right before you walked in seconds later. I'd had no idea he was there, and I was shocked you were there. I chased after you. I ran down the street in my towel, but you were gone."

"You chased after me? Wet and naked except for a towel in the snow?" Andrew looked at him wide-eyed.

"Yes," Connor said.

They stared at each other for a long moment.

"I'd chase you to the ends of the earth if I had to."

"Why?"

"Because, silly, I love you."

Andrew's heart swelled in his chest. He reached out and took Connor by the face, and kissed him. Andrew kissed him again and again. He kissed his eyelids, and he kissed the trails of tears. He tried to kiss away the hurt and the pain.

"I'm so sorry," Connor whispered between kisses.

"I'm sorry too," Andrew murmured.

Connor reached up and gently took Andrews's face in his strong hands. "You're all I have that is good and right in this world." His eyes opened, showing Andrew that he believed that to his core.

"You have so much more—"

"Not without you, I don't." Connor wrapped him in those strong arms. He nuzzled into his neck, tears mixed with tiny kisses.

"I need you," Andrew moaned.

"I need you too." Connor nodded rubbing his cheek against Andrews.

"No." Andrew nuzzled into Connor's neck and whispered, "I need you."

"Oh!"

Andrew dropped the blanket, and Connor had their shirts off in one fluid motion. Connor's strong hands felt every inch of him as he shoved the table to the side with his foot. Whiskey glasses clinked as they slid across the table, and Connor went to his knees, pulling down Andrew's sweat pants.

Connor took hold of Andrew, gave him a squeeze, and swallowed Andrew's cock almost to the base before he pulled off. "So fucking big," he murmured in appreciation and went down on him again. Andrew threw his head back, groaning. Beads of sweat broke out across his body as the fire burned hot, and he blazed hotter with every movement of him and Connor.

Connor worked his pants off but never released Andrew's cock. He pressed his own cock into Andrew's leg, and the friction made him moan. When Andrew tried to pull back, Connor grabbed him by the ass and pulled him back in.

Squeezing his tiny ass cheeks and pulling them open, one of Connor's fingers slid down to his hole and started circling it. Spitting on his hand, Connor rubbed it on that hole and inserted a finger, at which

Andrew gasped with pleasure. Andrew reached down, taking Connor by fistfuls of hair and face-fucking him. His heavy balls bounced against Connor's chin, and he raised a leg to prop on the table, allowing Connor's fingers to delve deeper into him.

"Oh fuck," Andrew moaned as he fucked into Connor's mouth and back onto his finger. "Oh, Connor—Oh, Connor!" He moaned louder as he started unloading into his boyfriend's mouth.

Connor swallowed every drop of jizz that exploded in his mouth until Andrew stopped and started to pull out.

Falling onto the couch, Andrew smiled at Connor as his lids started drooping.

"Amazing."

"Yes, you are." Connor caressed his legs and stomach, leaned in to kiss his navel, and then stood to retrieve the glasses. After getting them a refill, he sat down next to Andrew and pulled his naked body into him.

They lay together, watching the fire and drinking in silence for the next hour, when Andrew reached over and rubbed Connor's cock.

"You never did get off."

"I get off knowing I'm pleasing you." Connor smiled.

"Bullshit." Andrew laughed, stroking his hardening cock.

"You're going to wake it up, and then you'll be in a world of hurt," Connor teased.

"I'm counting on it."

Andrew leaned over, taking Connor in his mouth. Connor rubbed his back, enjoying the oral stimulation before his hand flowed down and cupped Andrew's tight little ass. He tapped a finger against Andrew's hole, eliciting a small moan, and then Connor wet his finger and inserted it into Andrew.

After a few moments, he inserted another finger and then pushed Andrew over onto his stomach, pulling on his hips until that little ass was sticking in the air just right. Leaning in, Connor put his tongue into that little hole. Andrew thrashed and moaned.

Climbing up behind him, Connor started to rub his cockhead against Andrew's tight, virgin hole. Andrew wiggled and started pushing back on him until Connor's cockhead slipped in.

"Oh, fuck." Andrew winced. "Hold up."

Connor held his position before leaning back to spit on his hand and rub it along his cock.

"It's not as big as yours," Connor joked.

"But it is bigger than your fingers," Andrew breathed, tense.

"Do you have lube? Or a condom?" Connor asked. "It will make it easier."

"I might have some lube in the car—"

"The car?" Connor's eyebrow raised in question.

"What? I was prepared to imagine fucking you as I pumped a load or three over holiday."

"At your parents?" Connor scrunched up his face.

"In my bed, or the shower, or with the stranger at the rest stop bathroom—"

"What?" Connor all but screamed.

"Too soon?" Andrew laughed. "I'll tell you about it when you're older."

"You can tell me now . . ."

"But your losing your, um," Andrew's eyes went from Connor's face to his cock and back again. "I mean, it happens when we get older—"

Connor landed a solid smack on Andrew's exposed cheek. "I'll be right back, and I'm going to show you what I can do with this—"

Connor jumped from the couch, crossed the room and into the cold, which was accompanied by Connor's calls of how cold it was. Returning to the house, muttering profane comments about how cold it was, he slammed the door.

"You didn't have to run into the freezing night naked, dumbass!"

"Young, dumb, hung," Connor smiled as he wiggled his hips. "And soon I'll be out of cum!"

"Oh?" Andrew laughed as Connor popped the lube top and gave a quick shake of his hips as he crossed the room.

"Hey, umm, I don't have a condom," Connor sat next to Andrew. "But I was just tested, and I can honestly say that you'll be the last man I ever sleep with."

Andrew stared deep into Connor's eyes.

"Okay," Andrew whispered silently.

"Yeah?"

Andrew leaned forward, kissing Connor deeply, moaning, "Oh, yeah."

Connor gently, firmly put Andrew back into the position he was in before. Connor place his cock at Andrew's entrance, and slowly pressed until he was inside. A grunt of confused pleasure with pain accompanied the crackling of the fire, and Andrew gripped the couch in his fist.

"Just relax," Connor encouraged soothingly. His voice was low and hypnotic. He leaned over Andrew's back, cupped his face in his hand, and turned Andrew until he was able to kiss him, taking his mind off the pain. After a while, he pushed slowly into him again until he was all the way in.

"Oh God," Andrew moaned into his mouth.

Wrapping an arm around his chest, Connor started to slowly fuck him with long, even strokes. Soon Andrew was pushing back to meet those strokes.

Connor looked down as his cock invaded his boyfriend, and he could feel his orgasm building. "I'm not going to last long," Connor moaned.

Pulling Andrew's hips up so he could get to his rock-hard cock, Connor smiled at what he found. "Again?"

"Don't judge me," Andrew moaned.

Gently but firmly, Connor started stroking Andrew as he fucked his ass faster and faster. Andrew began to moaning and fucking the fist around his cock and backed on and off the cock in him.

"I'm cumming," Andrew yelled as his cock spasmed. His ass held Connor in its tight, velvety grip, and the next plunge pushed him over the edge.

Connor unloaded into Andrew with each strong thrust until he fell onto Andrew's back.

"That was amazing," Connor whispered into Andrew's ear. "You are amazing." He rolled onto his side, pulled Andrew out from under him, and positioned him in front of him as a little spoon. After pulling the cover up to their hips, they fell asleep before the roaring fire.

Andrew woke up the next morning to a cold breeze and the voice of his grampa cackling, "Found 'em!"

"Thank heavens," his mom's voice echoed from beyond the porch.

"They'll need a few before you go a bargin' in on 'em." Grampa smiled as he closed the door.

The End

Leave a Review

If you enjoyed reading the story, please leave a review. All reviews help new authors get a feel for their readers, and it helps readers find new stories to love.

I appreciate the reviews and feedback! If you would leave a review by stars or comments at the end of the story to share on Amazon it would be much welcomed.

~Kelvin

You can join Kelvin on his Goodreads page at:

https://www.goodreads.com/author/show/40815582.Kelvin_Young

Follow on Facebook at:

Facebook

Follow Kelvin on X formerly known as Twitter:

Kelvin Young (@kelvin_young69) / X (twitter.com)

Other Works

Summer's Secret:

Book 1 of the Curious

Find it at: https://mybook.to/tU5a6

When the connections regarding 'true and 'false' blur--

Alaric is a respected lawyer who has it all: money, looks, and a sex drive to make the young envious. With his best friends Jerry and Nick by his side it couldn't get much better. . . Or could it?

Alaric's son Milo, and his friends, are home from university, and they are ready to party the summer away. Trying to find their way in the world, lines blur as they see what they want and stop at nothing to get it.

Alaric enjoys his macho straight world where he is an alpha, but it all comes crashing down when he stumbles upon his best friend's son with another man in the gym shower. Confusing thoughts take root and soon those thoughts manifest into actions.

But are those actions moral? Is this just an expression of desire in its most base form?

Alaric stumbles through the summer trying to find his truth. Along the way, he finds the true meaning of friendship, love, and loss. But when the end of summer reveals her secrets, Alaric's world will find new meaning.

Poles and Holes

An Erotic Short Series:

https://www.mybook.to/PnH

This is no ordinary cruise . . . This was a gay cruise . . .

Book 1 – Someone to Lose

Book 2 – Someone to Use

Book 3 – Someone to Spare

Book 4 – Someone to Share

Book 5 – Someone to Bare

Book 6 – Someone to Dare

Because everyone needs a little <u>me</u> time to reconnect with themselves . . .